P9-DCX-098

DISCARD

The Flimflam Affair

CARPENTER AND QUINCANNON MYSTERIES

The Flimflam Affair

A CARPENTER AND QUINCANNON MYSTERY

BILL PRONZINI

A TOM DOHERTY ASSOCIATES BOOK  NEW YORK

This is a work of fiction. All of the characters, organizations, and events portrayed in this novel are either products of the author's imagination or are used fictitiously.

THE FLIMFLAM AFFAIR

Copyright © 2018 by Pronzini-Muller Family Trust

A Forge Book
Published by Tom Doherty Associates
175 Fifth Avenue
New York, NY 10010

www.tor-forge.com

Forge® is a registered trademark of Macmillan Publishing Group, LLC.

Library of Congress Cataloging-in-Publication Data

Names: Pronzini, Bill, author.
Title: The flimflam affair / Bill Pronzini.
Description: First Edition. | New York : Forge, 2019. | "A Tom
    Doherty Associates Book."
Identifiers: LCCN 2018044766| ISBN 9780765394378 (hardcover) |
    ISBN 9780765394385 (ebook)
Subjects: | GSAFD: Mystery fiction.
Classification: LCC PS3566.R67 F6 2019 | DDC 813/.54—dc23
LC record available at https://lccn.loc.gov/2018044766

Our books may be purchased in bulk for promotional, educational, or business
use. Please contact your local bookseller or the Macmillan Corporate and
Premium Sales Department at 1-800-221-7945, extension 5442, or by email at
MacmillanSpecialMarkets@macmillan.com.

First Edition: January 2019

Printed in the United States of America

0 9 8 7 6 5 4 3 2 1

For those who enjoyed the previous

six books in the Carpenter and

Quincannon series

The Flimflam Affair

1

SABINA

Sabina was ten minutes early for her two o'clock appointment with Winthrop Buckley. She had decided to walk the relatively short distance from lower Market Street to the Montgomery Block where his offices were situated. There was no other pressing business to keep her at Carpenter and Quincannon, Professional Detective Services, and John had left the day before for Jamestown on an investigation for the Sierra Railway Company. It being a clear, crisp fall day, she set a brisk pace.

On the way she wondered again what had prompted Mr. Buckley to seek the services of a detective agency. His Telephone Exchange call earlier had been brief; he said only that it was a private matter of some importance. Well, she would find out soon enough. It was customary for a prospective client to come to the agency for a preliminary consultation, but he had a busy schedule and had sounded harried, so she agreed to the appointment with him. A citizen who could afford offices in the "Monkey

Block," that four-story haven of lawyers, financiers, physicians, writers, and artists, was likely to be the sort of well-to-do client John coveted.

Rather than dally in the shops on the ground-floor level, she went straight to the elevators, exited the car on the third floor, and stepped through the frosted-glass door marked C. E. BUCKLEY, SECURITIES INVESTMENT BROKERAGE. She expected to be asked to wait in the anteroom until two o'clock, but the receptionist immediately took her card into a private office, came back in no more than fifteen seconds, said, "Mr. Buckley will see you now, Mrs. Carpenter," and ushered her inside.

Winthrop Buckley in the flesh was something of a surprise. On the telephone his voice had been strong and a bit gruff, leading her to envision a large, imposing individual. He was, in fact, just the opposite—a short, slight, almost gnomish man of some fifty-odd years, his thinning crown of hair and neatly trimmed spade beard the color of faded red brick shot through with mortarlike streaks of gray. He peered at her somewhat myopically through gold-rimmed spectacles as he took her hand and thanked her for her prompt arrival. Despite his lack of stature, he exuded an air of forcefulness as befitted a successful investment broker.

His office, like the anteroom, was conservatively and functionally furnished. A large mahogany desk and comfortable leather chairs, all of good quality but nondescript in design, dark gray carpeting, unadorned walls flanking a pair of windows that overlooked Washington Street. Unlike some successful businessmen, Winthrop Buckley clearly considered it unnecessary to outfit his work environment with symbols of his prosperity.

When they were both seated, Sabina asked how she might be of service. Instead of answering he removed a business card similar to hers from his vest pocket, leaned forward to slide it across the polished surface of his desk. It was of plain white vellum engraved with black lettering:

UNIFIED COLLEGE OF THE ATTUNED IMPULSES
PROF. A. VARGAS
SPIRIT MEDIUM AND COUNSELOR

Sabina studied it for a moment before raising her head. Buckley was watching her expectantly, his breathing audible and a bit wheezily asthmatic. "Are either of those names familiar?" he asked.

"No, I'm afraid not."

"I was hoping they would be. Frankly, I don't know whether to be relieved or disappointed."

"Are you a follower of spiritualism, Mr. Buckley?"

"Reluctantly," he said. "In deference to my wife. She believes wholeheartedly in communication with the disembodied essences of the dead, what Professor Vargas refers to as 'spiritual vibrations of the positive and negative forces of material and astral planes.'"

"And you don't?"

"I am a practical man, and a skeptical one after thirty years in the securities business. No one has yet to convince me that the living can converse with the dead, especially not A. Vargas."

"You think he's a charlatan?"

"I hope not, for my wife's sake, but I suspect he may well be. If so, I will need positive proof in order to convince Margaret. That is why I wish to retain you."

Spiritualism was a growing movement in the United States, though as yet not as popular in San Francisco as it was in the East. While there were any number of psychics, crystal gazers, and palm readers operating in the city, most of them on Kearney Street on the edge of the Barbary Coast, Sabina knew of only three self-styled mediums, all women, who conducted séances and claimed to perform "spirit wonders." She had had no direct dealings with any of them, nor with any spiritualism-related fraud cases in Denver during her time as a "Pink Rose" operative for the Pinkerton Detective Agency, and she had never heard of Vargas or the Unified College of the Attuned Impulses. A new game in town, likely.

"How long has Professor Vargas been here in the city?" she asked.

"Only a short time. A little over two months. Margaret went to consult with him as soon as she learned of his so-called college." Mr. Buckley removed his spectacles, pinch-rubbed tired-looking brown eyes. Then he sighed and said, "My wife believes that it is possible to obtain an audience with our daughter Bernice, a childhood victim of diphtheria. None of the other mediums she has consulted was able to effect such a dubious contact. Professor Vargas, however, has managed to convince her that he can and will summon Bernice through his spirit guide."

"At a fee you consider exorbitant?"

"No, he charges only nominal fees. Refers to them as donations to the Unified College of Attuned Impulses. Ten dollars for an individual psychic consultation, twenty-five dollars per person for attendance at his séances. But he makes no secret of the fact that larger donations are not only welcomed but encouraged from satisfied acolytes."

"I take it he hasn't satisfied Mrs. Buckley as yet."

"No, but I am afraid he's capable of it."

"How often has she visited him?"

"Six private sittings and two séances thus far, the most recent séance two nights ago. I joined her then at her insistence."

"Were just the two of you present?"

"No, there was one other couple."

"Held where?"

"In a closed room in his place of residence. Quite a performance, I must say. Margaret was most favorably impressed, as were the other devotees. Even I found it remarkably well staged."

"What exactly took place?"

Mr. Buckley explained in terse detail. Vargas had ordered his "psychic assistant," a woman named Annabelle, to securely tie him to his chair, then he proceeded to invoke such apparently supernormal phenomena as bell-ringing, table-tipping, spirit lights, automatic writings, and ectoplasmic manifestations. As his finale he announced that he was being unfettered by his friendly spirit guide and guardian, Angkar, and the rope that had bound him was heard to fly through the air just before the lights were turned up; when examined by Buckley and the other attendees, the rope was completely free of the more than ten knots that had been tied into it.

Even though "unstable influences in the fourth dimension" had prevented the departed Bernice from putting in an appearance, Margaret Buckley had been impressed enough to return the next day without her husband's knowledge, to arrange for two more private audiences. And for her and her husband's presence at another séance this coming Saturday night, at which Vargas promised to do everything in his power to establish and maintain contact with the shade of the long-deceased daughter. Should such a connection come to pass, Mrs. Buckley was prepared to, as her husband put it to Sabina, "endow the damned . . . excuse me, the Unified College of the Attuned Spirits with five thousand dollars." Nothing Mr. Buckley had said or done had changed her mind. The only thing that would was a public unmasking of the professor as knave and charlatan, if in fact that was what he was.

Sabina said, "You mentioned that he holds his private audiences and conducts his séances in his place of residence. Where is it located?"

"On Turk Street, near Van Ness Avenue. A modest house, number 3106."

"Bought or rented?"

"I have no idea."

"Who else resides there? The psychic assistant you mentioned?"

"Evidently. A strange little woman, Annabelle."

"Strange in what way?"

"In appearance and actions both. She flits about wraithlike in a long black robe cowled like a monk's."

"Was anyone else on the premises?"

"Not that I saw."

"How would you describe Professor Vargas?"

"Dark complexion, curling black mustache, piercing black eyes. Speaks in a deep, powerful voice like that of an actor. Wears a robe similar to Annabelle's and a large white amulet identical to hers." Buckley added grudgingly, "An imposing figure."

"His age?"

"Relatively young. Thirty-five to forty, at a guess."

"Do you have any idea where he and Annabelle resided before moving here?"

"I asked Vargas that," Buckley said. "His answer was vague and evasive. 'The East' is all he would say."

"Did he give any indication of why he chose San Francisco?"

"Not to me. Or to Margaret."

"Who was the other couple at last Saturday's séance?"

"Dr. and Mrs. Oliver Cobb."

The name was unfamiliar to Sabina. "Medical doctor?"

"Yes. And like Margaret, both true believers. The doctor seeks to communicate with his mother, who died recently."

"Did you voice your misgivings to him or Mrs. Cobb?"

"No. Nor to Vargas. Only to my wife."

There was a discreet knock on the door, after which it opened just far enough for the receptionist to poke her blond head through. "Excuse me for interrupting, Mr. Buckley, but Mr. Archer is here."

"Yes, all right, tell him I'll be with him shortly." When the blond head withdrew and the door closed, Buckley said to Sabina, "Have you any more questions, Mrs. Carpenter?"

"Not at the moment, no."

"Then I must terminate this meeting—a crucial business matter. You will investigate Vargas and his activities?"

"Yes. I'll begin immediately."

"Good, good, thank you."

Buckley asked the amount of the fee, and when Sabina told him, he quickly wrote a check, blotted it, handed it to her, and rose to accompany her to the door. His handshake and good-bye were perfunctory, his mind already turned to whatever crucial business matter awaited him.

It wasn't until she was in the hallway outside C. E. Buckley, Securities Investment Brokerage, that Sabina looked at the check. Winthrop Buckley either had great faith in her abilities or had become too preoccupied with his upcoming meeting to realize what he was doing, for the amount was not merely the retainer sum she had named but two-thirds of the full fee, sans expenses, for a successfully completed investigation.

John would be delighted.

Before returning to Carpenter and Quincannon, Professional Detective Services, Sabina made two stops. The first was at the Miner's Bank on New Montgomery, where she deposited Mr. Buckley's generous check. The second was the Western Union office on Market Street. There, she wrote and sent three wires—one each to the offices of the Pinkerton Detective Agency in Chicago, New York, and Washington, D.C., requesting information on Professor A. Vargas and the Unified College of the Attuned Impulses. She included the capsule descriptions of Vargas and his assistant Annabelle. If the pair had ever run afoul of the law, the Pinks would have a dossier on them or be able to track down the requisite information.

At the agency, she prepared a file on the investigation and noted Buckley's payment in the accounts receivable ledger. Then she penned a message to Madame Louella, the Kearney Street fortune-teller who claimed to be a Transylvanian Gypsy (she had in fact been born in Ohio) and whose alternate profession was that of gatherer and seller of information involving the city's less savory elements. If anyone knew or could find out if A. Vargas was a professional flimflammer, it was a rival "psychic" who was one herself. Finished with the message, Sabina sealed it into an envelope and took it to the messenger delivery service a few doors down the block.

Busywork occupied the rest of the afternoon. She had no visitors and no one rang up through the Telephone Exchange. The office had an empty feel to it. She found herself wishing she had been able to talk Elizabeth Petrie into joining the firm on a regular basis; her company as well as her able assistance would have been welcome. But Elizabeth, the widowed former police matron who did part-time duty for them when needed, had been loath to give up her comfortable independence for full-time work.

The feeling of emptiness—or perhaps loneliness was a better word—was one Sabina had seldom experienced until the past few months. Always before during the five years of her partnership with John, she had missed him only slightly when he was away on business. Their relationship had been strictly professional, though he would have had it otherwise. He was a very good detective and quite capable of taking care of himself, despite a tendency toward rash behavior in certain circumstances; she hadn't worried about him, or at least very little. Now . . .

Now she did miss him, worry about his welfare; their connection had become personal as well as professional and he was more or less constantly in her thoughts. He had finally worn down her resistance, succeeded in convincing her that his intentions were honorable; and she in turn had come to realize she could no longer continue to devote herself to Stephen's memory after five years of widowhood, and to admit to herself that John was more than just partner and friend. The desperate, terrifying events of three months ago, about which she still had nightmares, had drawn them even closer together.

She had vowed to herself that she would not sleep with him unless he proposed marriage, but she was weakening on that point, too. Six years of celibacy was enough, more than enough; the erotic dreams she'd been having about John made that abundantly clear. Whether he proposed or not—and she thought he might be readying himself to do so—she was not sure she would be able to withhold her favors much longer.

Five o'clock finally came. She pinned on her hat, donned her cape, closed the office, and went to board the streetcar that would take her to her flat on Russian Hill. The flat, too, would have a lonely feel tonight, she knew, despite the presence of Adam and Eve. Cats were all well and good as pets, but no substitute for human company.

How long would John's investigation in the Jamestown area take? He'd thought only a few days, but he could be away as much as a week or more—and that seemed a long time. Sabina chided herself for being silly; she was, after all, an independent, emancipated woman engaged in a sometimes dangerous, male-dominated profession. But the chiding did no good. Tonight she felt needy, oddly vulnerable.

It was a mood that wouldn't linger, however, because she would not allow it to. Emotion could always be conquered by a strong will, and Sabina Carpenter was nothing if not strong-willed.

2

QUINCANNON

The four-car Sierra Railway train chuffed and wheezed into Jamestown just past one o'clock, more than an hour behind schedule. Quincannon was in a grumpy mood when he alighted from the forward passenger coach, traveling valise in hand, and stood vibrating slightly from the constant jouncing and swaying. The overnight trip from San Francisco, by way of Stockton and Oakdale, had been fraught with delays, the car had been overheated to ward off the late fall chill in these Mother Lode foothills, his head ached from all the soot and smoke he'd inhaled, and this was not yet his final destination. Another train ride, short and doubtless just as blasted uncomfortable, awaited him before the day was done.

The town's long, crooked main street stretched out beyond the depot. Two- and three-storied wood and stone buildings lined both sides—business establishments and professional offices on one, rows of saloons and Chinese washhouses on the other—and the street was packed with rough-garbed men and a variety of conveyances. Behind the saloons, hidden by tall cottonwoods, lay the notorious red-light district known as "Back-of-Town." Quincannon happened to know this by hearsay, not personal experience; this was his first visit to the Queen of the Mines. If he were fortunate, he thought irritably, it would also be his last.

Jimtown's long-standing reputation as the "rip-snortin'est, most altogether roughest town in the mines" was evidently justified. It certainly appeared to be far less tamed down than the mining communities of Grass Valley and Nevada City, seventy-some miles to the north, where he and Sabina had had the misfortune of visiting this past summer. A mad cacophony of noises bludgeoned his eardrums—whistles, cowbells, raucous shouts, tinny piano music, crowing roosters, braying mules, snorting horses, clanks and rattles and steam hisses in the rail yards, distant dynamite blasts and the constant pound of ore crushers at the Ophir and Crystalline mines on the southern outskirts. Those mines, and hundreds more within a ten-mile radius, had already reputedly produced some two million dollars of gold in this year of 1897. Little wonder that the small town was wide open and clamorous.

A reception committee of two awaited Quincannon in front of the depot. The middle-aged gent sporting skimpy brown side whiskers introduced himself as Adam Newell, Sierra Railway's chief engineer. The long and lanky one with fierce gray eyes and a mustache to match was Samuel B. Halloran, Jimtown's marshal.

The pair ushered Quincannon into a private office inside the depot, where a third man waited—heavyset, clean-shaven, dressed in a black broadcloth suit spotted with cigar ash and overlain with a gold watch chain as large as any Quincannon had ever seen. This was C. W. Cromarty, the railroad's division superintendent.

Cromarty's desk was stacked with profiles, cross-sections, and specification sheets for bridges and building materials such as rails, ties, and switches; arranged behind it was a series of drafting boards containing location and contour maps of the area. All of this, Quincannon was to learn, was for the continuation of the road's branch into Angels Camp. The branch had been completed as far as Tuttletown, where the trouble that had brought him here had taken place three nights ago.

After they had shaken hands, Cromarty said, "We'll make this conference brief, Mr. Quincannon. A freight is due in from Tuttletown any minute. As soon as it arrives, we'll leave in my private car."

That was fine by Quincannon; the sooner the second jolting train ride commenced, the sooner it would end. He produced his stubby briar and pouch of Navy Cut, began thumbing tobacco into the blackened bowl.

"Has any new information come to light on the robbery?" he asked.

"None so far."

The engineer, Newell, said, "Tuttletown's constable, George Teague, would have sent word if he'd learned anything. He's a good man, Teague, but out of his element in a matter such as this. We'll be relying on you, sir."

"A well-placed reliance, I assure you."

"Pretty sure of yourself, ain't you?" Halloran said around the stub of a slender cheroot. His voice and his expression both held a faint sneer.

"With just cause."

"That remains to be seen. You may have a fancy-pants reputation as a detective in San Francisco, you and that woman of yours, but you don't cut no ice up here."

Quincannon bristled at this—literally. When his ire was aroused, the hairs in his dark freebooter's beard stiffened and quivered like the quills on a porcupine. He fixed the marshal with an eye fiercer than Halloran's own. "Sabina Carpenter is my partner, not 'my woman.'" *Not yet anyway.* "A Pinkerton-trained detective the equal of any man."

"So you say. Me, I never put much stock in a man that'd partner up with a female, trained or not."

"And I put no stock at all in one who blathers about matters he knows nothing about."

Cromarty said, "Here, that'll be enough of that. Marshal, this is a railroad matter, as you well know. The decision to engage Mr. Quincannon has been made and will be abided by."

"I still say I can do a better job than some citified puff-belly."

Quincannon bit back a venomous retort. A substantial fee to fatten the bank account of Carpenter and Quincannon, Professional Detective Services, had been requested in his reply to Cromarty's first wire, and agreed upon in his second. It wouldn't do to indulge in an angry sparring match with a small-town peacekeeper who had no say in the matter and no jurisdiction outside his own bailiwick.

He made a point of ignoring Halloran while he snicked a

match alight and fired his pipe. When it was drawing to his satisfaction, he said to Cromarty, "Now then, Superintendent—suppose you provide the details of the robbery left out of your wire. What exactly was the contents of the safe that was stolen?"

"Ten thousand dollars in gold dust and bullion from two of the mines near Tuttletown, awaiting shipment here and on to Stockton."

"A considerable sum. Why was it being kept in the express office overnight?"

"The shipment failed to arrive in time for the last train that afternoon. The Tuttletown agent felt no cause for concern."

"Damn fool," Halloran muttered.

"No, I don't blame Booker. We all believed the gold was secure where it was. What we overlooked was the audacity of thieves who would carry off a four-hundred-pound burglarproof safe in the middle of the night."

Quincannon said, "Burglarproof?"

"A brand-new model, guaranteed as such by the manufacturer."

"I've heard such guarantees before."

"This one has been proven to our satisfaction. Sierra Railway Express now uses them exclusively."

"What brand of safe is it?"

Cromarty said, "Cannon Berch, with a circular door of reinforced steel. The dial and spindle can be removed once the combination is set, and when that has been done, the safe is virtually impenetrable and indestructible. Not even the most accomplished cracksman was able to breach it in the manufacturer's tests."

"And the dial and spindle were removed in this case?"

"Yes. Booker did that before he locked up, took them home with him. He still has them and swears they were never out of his sight."

"Virtually impenetrable and indestructible, you said? Even with explosives? Dynamite or nitroglycerin inserted in the dial hole in the door?"

"Can't be done," Newell said. "You couldn't open a dialless Cannon Berch with a pile driver."

Quincannon remained dubious. Ingenuity could be a two-edged sword, as he well knew from experience. If a so-called burglarproof safe could be built, a way to breach it could like-wise be found.

"Is this fact common knowledge locally?" he asked.

"I wouldn't say common knowledge," Cromarty said, "but we've made no secret of the fact."

Then why had the thieves—thieves, plural, for it would have taken at least two strong men to transport four hundred pounds of gold-filled steel—broken into the express office and made off with the safe? Half-wits who refused to believe "burglarproof" and yielded to temptation? Professional yeggs? The latter seemed unlikely, for how would they have known of the availability of both safe and gold in this remote area?

A large, heavy wagon would have been required to spirit the safe away from the Tuttletown depot, but there was no potential clue in that fact; ore and freight wagons plied the area in large numbers. Nor was there any way to tell in which direction the plunder had been taken, or how far. Two main roads crossed at Tuttletown, one running northward to Angels Camp, the other southward toward Stockton, and there were also a number of intermediate roads connecting with other Mother Lode communities. The town had been the hub of mining activity since placer days, surrounded by a cluster of settlements so close that pioneers from Jackass Hill, Mormon Gulch, and half a dozen others on the west side of Table Mountain could walk into Tuttletown to shop.

These facts had made the town a prime target for thieves before. In the seventies and early eighties, the notorious poetry-spouting bandit known as Black Bart had filched three Wells, Fargo stage shipments of bullion and dust amounting to five thousand dollars from the nearby Patterson mine. Quincannon had been with the Secret Service on the East Coast at that time—it was not until 1885 that he had been transferred west to the Service's San Francisco office—so he'd had no opportunity to pit his detective skills against Black Bart's criminal wiles. If he had, he'd once confided to Sabina, he would surely have been the one to put an end to the bandit's criminal career.

Outside, a distant train whistle sounded. One long, mournful blast, followed closely by a second.

"That's the Tuttletown freight, Mr. Quincannon," Cromarty said. "We'll take our departure as soon as the main tracks are clear."

The superintendent's private car waited on a siding at the near end of the rail yards, coupled to a Baldwin 4-4-0 locomotive. Cromarty, Newell, and Quincannon were the only passengers. Halloran had left them at the depot to return to his marshal's duties, with a parting remark about cocksure flycops that Quin-cannon pretended not to hear. When he resolved this stolen safe business, he vowed to himself, he would not leave Jimtown until he looked up Samuel B. Halloran and claimed the last word.

The car appeared ordinary enough on the outside, but the in-terior was well appointed with upholstered chairs and settee, a brace of tables, and a private sleeping compartment. It also con-tained a ceiling fan and a sheet-iron stove. The comfort, plus a late lunch once they were under way, improved Quincannon's disposition considerably.

The Angels Camp extension branched off Sierra's main line in front of the Neville Hotel, bridged a creek at the north end of town, then climbed a steep grade to a cut high on Table Moun-tain. Over on the mountain's west side, the tracks swept down another steep grade and curved around a wide valley and several working mines before swinging northward into Tuttletown. The place was a smaller but no less busy and noise-ridden version of Jamestown, its narrow streets, stores, and saloons clogged with off-shift miners and railroad workers from the crews engaged in laying new track and constructing what Cromarty described as a "fifty-foot-high, seventeen-bent wooden trestle" across the Stanislaus River to the north.

A one-man reception committee awaited them here. As soon as the Baldwin hissed to a stop, Quincannon, looking through the window, saw a round, balding man emerge from under the platform roof and hurry over to the car. He was waiting when the three men stepped down, mopping his moon face with a ban-dana. Despite the fact that the day was cool and overcast, he was sweating profusely.

Cromarty said, "Hello, Booker," which marked him as the Tuttletown express agent, Howard Booker. "This is John Quincannon, the detective I sent for. Where's Constable Teague?"

Booker said excitedly, "I got news, Mr. Cromarty. Big news. The safe's been found."

"Found, you say? When? Where?"

"About an hour ago. In a field off Icehouse Road. Teague's out there now with the rancher who found it."

"Splendid! Abandoned by the thieves, eh?"

"Abandoned, all right, but the news ain't splendid."

"What do you mean?"

"Turns out that burglarproof safe's no such thing," Booker said. "She's been opened somehow and she's empty. The gold's gone."

3

QUINCANNON

Icehouse Road, obviously named after a native-stone building with ICE painted on its facing wall that squatted alongside a broad creek, serpentined away from town into the hilly countryside. The buggy that Booker had had waiting for them bounced through chuckholes and over thick-grassed hummocks. A grim-visaged C. W. Cromarty sat up front with the express agent, Quincannon on the backseat with Newell. All four kept their own counsel on the quarter-mile ride.

Around a bend, a broad meadow opened up near where the road forked ahead. Scrub oak and manzanita, and outcroppings of rock, spotted the high grass. A buckboard and a saddled chestnut gelding partially blocked the road, and under one of the larger oaks some twenty rods away, a group of three men stood waiting.

One of the men, a leaned-down gent with a handlebar mustache, detached himself from the others and hurried out to meet the rig. The star pinned to his cowhide vest identified him as the local constable, George Teague. He said to Cromarty, "Damnedest thing you ever saw, Mr. Cromarty. Just the damnedest thing. I couldn't hardly believe my eyes."

"Who found the safe?"

"Ben Higgins. He's a dairy rancher lives farther out this way."

Quincannon asked, "Has anything else been discovered in the vicinity?"

"Just a line of trampled grass," Teague said. "Looks like the safe was carried in from the road." He paused, studying Quincannon with his head cocked slightly to one side as if he suffered from a stiff neck. "You the detective from San Francisco?"

Cromarty answered the question and introduced them. Then he said in bleak tones, "Very well. Let's have a look at it."

They trooped through the grass to where the other two men—the rancher, Higgins, and Teague's deputy—waited. The safe lay tilted on its side in the oak's shade, one corner dug deep into the grassy earth. The black circular door, bearing the words SIERRA RAILWAY EXPRESS in gold leaf above the manufacturer's name, was open and partially detached, hanging by a single bolt from a bent hinge. Cromarty and Newell stood staring down at it, mouths pinched tight. Quincannon stepped past them, lowered himself to one knee for a closer examination.

"She wasn't blowed open," Teague said behind him. "You can see that plain enough."

Quincannon could. There were no powder marks on the door or other evidence that explosives had been used, nor did the center hold for the dial and spindle show any damage. Yet the door had clearly been forced somehow; the bolts were badly twisted.

There were small gouge marks along the bottom edges of the door, the sort a wedge or chisel struck by sledgehammers would make, but a safe of this construction could not have been ripped open in that fashion, by brute force.

A whitish residue adhered to the steel along where the wedge marks were located. Quincannon scraped it with a thumbnail, rubbed it between thumb and index finger. Hard, flaky.

"What's that?" Newell asked.

"Dried putty, from the look and feel of it."

"Putty? What the devil could that have been used for?"

Quincannon gave no response. He was looking at another substance that had dried on the safe, on a corner of the door and on one of the outer sides—brownish smears of what was certainly dried blood.

Teague had spotted it before their arrival. He said, "One of 'em must've gashed hisself when they busted into the express office. And again when they got her open. There's blood on the floor inside, too."

Again Quincannon said nothing. Something else had drawn his attention, a piece of straw caught on one of the skewed bolts. He plucked it loose. Ordinary straw, clean and damp.

He leaned forward to peer inside the safe. Completely empty—not a gram of gold dust or speck of the other variety remained. He ran fingertips over the smooth walls and floor, found them to be cold and faintly moist. The dampness of metal and straw could have been the result of the safe having lain here in the open since last night, assuming that was when it had been dumped; but if that were the case, it should have dried by now, the day, though overcast, holding no indication of moisture.

When he straightened, Cromarty asked him, "Have you any idea how it was done?"

"Not as yet."

"If I weren't seeing it for myself, I wouldn't believe it. A guaranteed burglarproof safe . . . it just doesn't seem possible."

Quincannon suppressed a darkly pleased smile. Actions and events that didn't seem possible were his meat. There was nothing he liked better than the challenge of feasting on crimes that baffled and flummoxed average men and average detectives.

"Leave the safe here, Mr. Cromarty, or take it back to town?" Teague asked.

"Leave it for now. We'll send some men out for it later. Unless you'd rather have it brought in for further study, Mr. Quincannon?"

"Not necessary. I've seen enough of it."

Higgins had no useful information to impart. He had spied the safe as he was driving past in his wagon, he said, and stopped to investigate; no one else had been in the vicinity. A search of the area where the safe had been dumped provided no additional clues. The ground was too hard beneath the trampled grass here and in the section of meadow between the oak and the road to retain identifiable footprints.

The men rode back into Tuttletown. At the depot, Quincannon asked to have a look at the scene of the robbery both inside and out. Teague and Booker accompanied him to the rear of the old wood-frame building that housed the baggage and express office.

A small grove of poplars grew close together near the door on that side; under the cloak of late-night darkness, a wagon could easily have been drawn up under them and be well hidden in their shadows while the safe was removed. The jumbled tracks of men, wagons, and horses told Quincannon nothing illuminating, however.

He stepped up on the platform to look at the door. Its bolt lock had been forced with a pinch bar or similar instrument. As old and rusty as it was, it wouldn't have taken more than a few seconds for such to have been done.

Booker said, "There's a wood crossbar on the door inside, but they got it free somehow. It was on the floor when I come in yesterday morning."

There was no mystery as to how that had been accomplished. Once the bolt had been snapped, the thieves had pried a gap between the door edge and jamb just wide enough to slip a thin length of metal through and lift the crossbar free. Whoever they were, they were resourceful and determined.

Quincannon tried the door, found it secure; naturally Booker had replaced the crossbar. He asked the agent to go inside and remove it. While Booker was obliging, Quincannon studied the broken lock, the gouged wood, the crusted brown stains on the door edge. A fair amount of blood had been lost during the robbery; there were spatters on the platform as well. And more on the rough wood floor inside, he saw when Booker let him inside.

That much was clear. What was puzzling was the blood inside the safe. How had it come to be there *after* the alleged burglarproof box had been breached?

A dusty square in one corner outlined where the safe had

stood. It had been bolted to the floor, the rust-flecked bolts pried loose with the same instrument that had been used on the rear door. Still more dried blood stained the boards here.

Teague stood watching in his stiff-necked fashion. "You know, I looked the place over pretty good myself," he said. His patience seemed to be wearing thin. "Damn thieves didn't leave nothing of theirselves behind, else I'd've found it."

Nothing except for the blood, Quincannon thought but didn't say.

"If you ask me," Booker said, "the ones that done it are long gone by now. And the gold with 'em."

"Possibly. And possibly not."

"Well, they dumped the empty safe, didn't they? What reason would they have for sticking around?"

"Strong ties to the community, mayhap."

"Here, now," Teague said. "You saying you think they're locals?"

"Just speculating at this point, Constable. If they are locals, it stands to reason the gold is still in the vicinity as well."

"Even if you're right, that don't put us any closer to finding out who they are."

"Or how they got that safe open," Booker said. "Dynamite wasn't used and they couldn't of done it with hammers and chisels."

"Nor a pile driver," Quincannon said wryly, echoing Newell's words in Jamestown.

"Then how in bloody hell did they manage it?"

"The *how* and the *why* may well be linked. The answer to one question will provide the answer to the other."

"Well now, mister," Teague said, "that sounds like double-talk to me. Ain't no shame in admitting you're as fuddled as the rest of us."

No shame in it if it were true, but it wasn't. Quincannon prided himself that he was never fuddled, at least not for very long.

Teague mistook his silence for tacit agreement. "So then how're you gonna go about finding the answers?"

"A detective never reveals his methods until his investigation is complete," Quincannon said. And sometimes, he added silently, not even then.

Dusk had begun to settle when he left the express office. Cromarty had issued an invitation to dine with him and Newell and to spend the night in his private car, but Quincannon preferred a solitary environment and his own company when he was in the midst of a case. He went first to Tuttletown's only hostelry, the Cremer House—the best room the hotel had to offer, which turned out to be cramped, spartanly furnished, and stuffy. He stayed in it just long enough to deposit his valise and open the single window partway.

Downstairs again, he asked the elderly desk clerk, "Does Tuttletown have a doctor?"

"Why? You feeling poorly?"

Quincannon ignored the question. "*Is* there a doctor here?"

"There is. Doc Goodfellow."

"Where does he reside?"

"Home and office above the dry-goods store, one block east. But you won't find him there."

"No? Why not?"

"Cave-in up at the Rappahanock mine a couple hours ago. They were still digging out the injured when one of the men come for the doc. Likely he'll be up there most of the night."

Quincannon didn't bother asking the clerk how he knew about the accident; word traveled swiftly in small towns such as this, especially word of a sudden tragedy. Nor did he answer a second query about the state of his health. His business with Dr. Goodfellow was none of the clerk's.

Just down the street from the hotel he spied a place labeled the Miners Rest Café. He made it his next stop—and wasted half an hour on an unsatisfactory dinner. A bowl of mulligan stew was watery and oversalted, and a pie made with vinegar and raisins—a Mother Lode country favorite, the waitress informed him—was about as appetizing as its name, fly pie. You would think an eatery that catered to miners would have better fare, but then most of the town's business establishments were saloons and dance halls—testimony to the fact that liquor, beer, and the usual free lunches claimed most of the hardrock business.

A brisk stroll around the crowded, noisy town aided his digestion and eliminated the last of the muscle kinks from two days of train travel. When he'd had enough of the mountain night's chill and the constant throbbing of the stamps, he made the rounds of the watering holes to see if he could pick up any useful scuttlebutt.

As he'd anticipated, there were two main topics of conversation: the mine cave-in, and the robbery and mysterious cracking of the burglarproof safe. The consensus of opinion among the rough-garbed locals about the latter event seemed to be that one of the gangs of gold thieves that roamed these foothills was responsible; if anyone knew anything to the contrary, he kept it to himself. These men were naturally suspicious of outsiders, and the fact that Quincannon was a San Francisco detective had as quickly become common knowledge as the Rappahanock mine cave-in. He was recognized as soon as he entered each saloon, and mostly given a wide berth and ignored. None of the few patrons he approached would discuss the robbery with him, not even for the price of a drink.

He was neither dismayed nor disappointed. The effort had been a long shot at best; it was unlikely that he would be given assistance from any quarter in his investigation, voluntary or otherwise. Not that he would need it. His canny brain was busily piecing together the clues already in his possession, and while a pattern had yet to emerge, he was confident that one would.

Weary now, he returned to Cremer House and stretched out on the lumpy bed in his room. One of the temperance tracts he carried with him on trips—the perfect soporific—put him to sleep before he had turned two pages.

4

SABINA

The house at 3601 Turk Street was a modest affair, its slender front yard enclosed by a black iron picket fence. Rented, not purchased, Sabina judged from the TO LET sign on the gate of one of its similar neighbors. No electrical power lines serviced it; Professor A. Vargas, particularly if he were a clever swindler, would have been careful to select a home that had not been wired for electricity. The sometimes spectral trembles produced by gas flame would be much more suited to his purpose.

On the gate here was a discreet bronze sign whose raised letters gleamed faintly in the cold morning sunshine. The wording was the same as that on the card Winthrop Buckley had shown her: UNIFIED COLLEGE OF THE ATTUNED IMPULSES, PROF. A. VARGAS, SPIRIT MEDIUM AND COUNSELOR.

She adjusted her plain black suit jacket, straightened the black lace-trimmed hat perched atop her dark hair which she'd pinned back into a bun—an effective mourning outfit missing only a veil she had decided was unnecessary. Then she climbed the short flight of stairs to the front door, twisted the bell handle.

Several seconds passed before the door opened. The small woman who stood facing her was also a study in black: coal-black eyes, straight ebon hair (dyed?) wound in a coronet above a high forehead, a sleek satin dress that had a sheen like polished onyx. Very pale skin gave her an appropriately ghostly aspect, enhanced by a white amulet embossed with some sort of cabalistic design nestled between ample breasts. For all of that, she was attractive in a severe fashion. Annabelle, surely, minus the cowled robe she apparently wore only at séances. If she did in fact live here with Vargas, she was likely his wife or mistress as well as his assistant. Seeking communion with the Afterworld, Sabina thought cynically, did not preclude indulging in the pleasures of the earthly sphere.

The ebon eyes took her measure. Not quite calculatingly, though the gaze did not miss the fact that her mourning outfit had come from a quality apparel shop. "Yes?"

Sabina had adopted a somewhat nervous, timid expression. She cleared her throat before she said, "I've come seeking an audience with Professor Vargas. I understand he has the power to communicate with those who have passed over."

"There is someone in the spirit world you wish to speak to?" The woman's voice was low-pitched, almost sepulchral.

"My brother. He died quite suddenly last week, you see, and I . . . well, I would very much like to communicate with him if at all possible."

"Your name?"

"Mrs. Dorothy Milford."

"I am Annabelle, Professor Vargas's psychic assistant. Enter and follow me, please."

Sabina trailed her down a murky hallway into a somewhat more brightly lighted parlor. Annabelle relieved her of her wrap, which she hung on a coat tree. "I will see if the professor is finished with his morning meditation," she said then. The satin dress rustled as she left the room through a wide black curtain at the far end.

Sabina remained standing, looking around the parlor. This was not where the séances were held, evidently. The only mediumistic trapping in the otherwise conventionally furnished room was the black curtain, which bore a larger version of the same "magic" symbol as that on the woman's amulet. Both curtain and symbol, Sabina noted, were somewhat similar to those that adorned Madame Louella's fortune-telling parlor.

Her wait was of less than five minutes' duration. The curtain parted again and Annabelle stepped through. "Professor Vargas has consented to grant you an audience, Mrs. Milford. A donation of ten dollars to the Unified College of the Attuned Impulses is customary for each private sitting."

"Oh, yes, of course. Shall I pay now?"

"After your consultation. Follow me, please."

Annabelle conducted her through the curtain, down another gloomy hallway, and through yet another curtain into a semidarkened room strongly scented with incense. Sabina, who hated the stuff, immediately began to breathe through her mouth. The only light came from two sources: a pair of white candles in pewter holders on the mantelpiece above a small fireplace—wisps of smoke emanated from the incense burner set between them—and a circular, glass-topped table in the middle of the room. The glass was opaque, and it was lighted within in some sort of phosphorescent manner; its glow and that of the flickering candles had the intended eerie effect in the shadowed surroundings. A high-backed, thronelike chair was placed on one side of the table, a pair of smaller armchairs arranged opposite. Cabalistically imprinted black drapes covered two walls; the other two, papered above dark wainscoting, were bare.

Annabelle announced to the man standing next to the chair, "Mrs. Dorothy Milford," and took her leave in a satiny whisper.

The man stepped forward, his hand extended. He, too, was dressed all in black except for a dark blue shirt and a twin of Annabelle's white amulet. Winthrop Buckley had referred to him as imposing, a description that Sabina, who was seldom impressed by physical stature, had to admit was apt. Tall, well built, with a mane of black hair and a vaguely Mephistophelean countenance. The only false note was his curled black mustache. It was no doubt meant to enhance his image, but it reminded her of the sort villains in stage melodramas wore. She hoped he wouldn't twirl the ends of his; she would be hard-pressed not to laugh if he did.

"Good morning, Mrs. Milford," he said in rich stentorian tones. The touch of his hand was light, almost feathery. It seemed to Sabina that he maintained the contact somewhat longer than necessary.

"Thank you for seeing me, Professor Vargas."

"I am always happy to serve one who believes in the spirit world. You are a sincere believer, I trust?"

"Oh, yes."

"Splendid. New friends are always welcome at the Unified College of the Attuned Impulses. How did you learn of us?"

"From Mr. Winthrop Buckley."

"Ah. Mr. Buckley's wife is a particularly ardent devotee."

"Yes, he told me."

"Have you consulted a spirit counselor before?"

"No. Only a clairvoyant on occasion."

Vargas nodded, smiling as he moved one of the smaller chairs close to the table across from the high-backed one. He held it for Sabina until she was seated, then moved around opposite. The seat on his chair was set slightly higher, so that when he perched he gave the oracular effect of looking down at her from a height.

Before he could speak, Sabina said, "I understand you have been in San Francisco only a short time, Professor. Did you establish the Unified College elsewhere?"

"Yes. Many years ago."

"May I ask where?"

"In the East."

"Chicago? New York?"

"I have shared my gift of spirit counseling with many believers in many locales," Vargas said glibly and evasively. He leaned forward, the light illuminating his dark features and giving his eyes a hypnotic shine. "Now then, shall we begin?"

"By all means," Sabina said. More questions would only make him suspicious.

"My assistant informed me that you seek to communicate with a loved one who has recently crossed the Rubicon."

"My brother Gregory. There are certain . . . pressing questions he left unanswered."

"The nature of those questions?"

"They regard our family finances. Investments . . . stocks, bonds, and the like."

Was that a glint of avarice in Vargas's penetrating gaze? It was difficult to be sure in the eerie table glow. "You are now in charge of these investments?" he asked.

Sabina said, "Yes, with the aid of our attorneys. But Gregory made all the decisions, you see, very profitable ones, and I don't wish to carry on with anything he might not approve of."

"Ah, I see."

"It *is* possible for you to summon him?"

"All things are possible in the realm of the spirit world. But it is not I who may summon him, but Angkar. I am merely a teacher of the light and truth of theocratic unity, merely a humbly blessed operator between the Beyond and this mortal sphere."

"Angkar?"

"My spirit guide. He lived more than a thousand years past and his spirit has ascended to one of the highest planes in the Afterworld."

"A Hindu, was he?"

"No, an Egyptian nobleman in the court of Nebuchadnezzar."

That statement was the first bit of proof that Professor A. Vargas was a charlatan, and a less than thorough one in his researches. For Nebuchadnezzar had not been an Egyptian, Sabina knew from her world history lessons as a girl, but the king of Babylon and conqueror of Jerusalem some six centuries B.C. She refrained from mentioning the fact, of course, though if she had, Vargas no doubt would have covered his mistake by claiming he'd meant Nefertiti or some such.

He placed both hands on the table in such a way that enormous rings on each of the middle fingers glittered in the light. They were of intricate design and bore hieroglyphics similar to those on the amulets. Sabina had the impression that he had displayed them deliberately for her inspection.

She said obligingly, "Are your rings Egyptian, Professor?"

"This one is." Vargas lifted his left hand. "An Egyptian signet and seal talisman ring, made from virgin gold." He presented his right hand. "This is the Ring of King Solomon. Its Chaldaic inscription stands as a reminder to the wearer that no matter what his troubles may be, they shall soon be gone. The inscription— here—translates as 'This shall also pass.'"

"Yes, as my brother's troubles have," Sabina said in feigned consternation. "How long will it take for Angkar to summon him?"

"That is a question I cannot answer at this time, Mrs. Milford. I must first have more information about your dear departed brother. Then in order to connect with the discarnate, I must place myself in a metagnomic trance and seek to inform Angkar of your desire to speak with Gregory's astral spirit."

My, my, Sabina thought wryly. Metagnomic trance. Another mistake, though most of Vargas's disciples would have been too captivated by his facile patter to have realized it. Metagnomy was not a type of trance, but a form of clairvoyance in which a sensitive supposedly could see the future while mesmerized. His research had been shoddy indeed.

She said, "I understand you will be conducting a séance here on Saturday night. Would it be possible for me to attend?"

"Certainly. I advise that you do."

"Then it's possible that you . . . I mean Angkar can summon Gregory's spirit at the sitting?"

"Possible, yes, if Gregory is among our many friends on the astral plane and your impulses are properly attuned so that a zone beyond spatial and temporal laws may be entered and a rapport thus established. But I cannot promise that contact will be made so quickly. That is Angkar's province, not mine."

"I feel that my impulses are already attuned with Gregory's. We were very close, you see."

"I have no doubt," Vargas said. "But that may not be the case now that Gregory's spirit resides in the Afterworld. The ways of spirit life are not those of earth life. We cannot truly understand the discarnate, for only small portions of the Great Mystery are revealed to mortals through the powerful presence of spirit guides such as Angkar."

More gobbledygook designed to fool the gullible. "How do I properly attune my impulses?"

"With my guidance. May I have your hand, please?"

"My hand?"

"As a sensitive, I am often able to determine the strength of one's impulses by means of spiritual contact."

Sabina let him take her hand again. He held it for a moment, then very gently began to stroke it, first the backs of her fingers, then her palm. His touch was light, caressing, all the while his gaze holding hers.

Spiritual contact, my eye! This definitely was not impersonal hand-holding; it was intimate and subtly sexual, as if he were testing her willingness to respond. A. Vargas was after more than just money from attractive female acolytes, by heaven—a rake as well as a fake.

She didn't let him get away with it for long. She withdrew her hand and said coolly, "And are my impulses strong, Professor?"

"They are," he said through one of his unctuous smiles. "Quite strong, indeed. However, inasmuch as Saturday's séance will be your first, I suggest one or two additional audiences in order for me to do everything in my power to prepare you."

And attempt to seduce me if you think I might be willing.

"Is that agreeable, Mrs. Milford?"

"Oh, yes," she lied.

"You understand that it may take several sittings before Gregory is summoned and you are able to speak with him?"

"As many as necessary," she lied again.

"Splendid." Vargas once more leaned forward into the light, his gaze still fixed unblinkingly on hers. "Now please be so kind as to tell me about your brother and his earthly activities."

Sabina had prepared a detailed family and business history, which she proceeded to unroll. Vargas asked several questions, not a few of them designed to elicit information about the wealth of the alleged Milford clan. The only truism was the name of the "family attorney," Archibald Maguire, who was in fact a prominent San Francisco lawyer. Maguire was counsel for cousin Callie and her husband, Hugh French, as well as Carpenter and Quincannon, Professional Detective Services. He had been amenable to assisting her and John in the course of their investigations in the past (for a fee, of course), and so she would arrange with him to corroborate her fabricated story about the Milfords in the event Vargas should decide to check up on it.

When the professor had gleaned all the data she was willing to provide, he commenced his "preparations." These were necessary, he said, not only to properly attune her impulses, but to guard against "malevolent forces" that sought to prevent communication with friendly spirits. The process consisted of a great deal of additional mumbo-jumbo about theocratic unity between the living and the dead and the nature of the astral plane so far as he claimed knowledge of it. Sabina pretended to listen attentively and to agree to everything he told her to do, except for acceding to another attempt to fondle her hand. That she firmly resisted.

Predictably the initial sitting concluded with Vargas urging once again that she come twice more before Saturday's séance. If he were successful in summoning Angkar, which of course he would be, he would tell her at their next meeting, and continue with her preparations according to the spirit guide's instructions. Her role as eager and submissive believer demanded consent; she must do nothing that might plant even a tiny worm of suspicion in Vargas's mind. But the prospect of two more visits to this dark, incense-laden room, and of having to continue to fend off his subtle advances while listening to his glib nonsense, was unpleasant in the extreme.

Vargas used some sort of hidden device to summon Annabelle, for she appeared abruptly through the curtain. Another too lengthy handshake and a silent bow ended the audience. Annabelle conducted her back to the parlor, where Sabina handed the woman a ten-dollar gold piece without being asked. She was then shown to the front door. All very swiftly and smoothly done, the result no doubt of long practice.

Outside, she drew several deep breaths of cold, fresh air. That helped rid her nostrils of the incense residue. But she continued to sniff its lingering smoky odor on her clothing on the streetcar ride downtown.

5

SABINA

First stop: the Geary Street suite belonging to Maguire and Sullivan, Attorneys at Law. Archibald Maguire was in court today, so Sabina met with his junior partner, a reliable man named Conroy, and told him of the Milford subterfuge. He said he would notify Mr. Maguire upon his return, and that he would alert the other members of the staff to refer any inquiries to him or to Mr. Maguire.

Next stop: the Western Union office on Market. One wire in response to hers of the day before had been delivered in her absence, from the Pinkerton office in Chicago. They knew nothing of the Unified College of the Attuned Impulses, a medium named A. Vargas and a woman called Annabelle, or anyone involved in the spirit racket answering their general descriptions. Either Vargas had never practiced his spiritualism dodge in the Windy City, or if he had, had never had a brush with the law. It was also possible that it was a relatively new undertaking. The research mistakes he'd made indicated that it might be, though he did seem to have put a reasonable polish on the rest of his game.

At the agency, Sabina added a detailed report of her meeting with Vargas and her impressions of him and Annabelle to the Buckley case file. There was little question in her mind that the pair was out to bilk as much money as possible from wealthy believers such as Margaret Buckley. But her professional opinion was not sufficient; proof was required before she presented her findings to the client. Saturday night's séance, with both Winthrop Buckley and his wife in attendance, might well provide that proof.

She was familiar with some of the tricks employed by fraudulent mediums, though not all. It was too bad John was away; he might well have acquired knowledge to augment hers. If he should return from the southern Mother Lode in time, she would ask him to accompany her to the séance. He might grumble and growl a bit, but the chance to expose a bunco scheme would persuade him. His dislike of grifters who preyed on the honest and gullible was as great as hers.

When she finished updating the file, she was surprised to note that it was nearly two o'clock. How quickly time passed. And another day in which work had distracted her enough to miss a noon meal. She would treat herself to an early tea shop dinner, she decided, after close of business.

First things first, however. She locked the office and took herself to the library to see what might be learned about the tricks of phony spiritualists.

The library possessed a number of books, pamphlets, and

treatises on spiritualism. All but two of these were staunchly supportive, among them Emma Hardinge Britten's *Nineteenth Century Miracles: Spirits and Their Work in Every Country of the Earth,* and the London Spiritualist Alliance's "Journal Devoted to the Highest Interests of Humanity, Both Here and Hereafter."

The less informative of the skeptical items was a pamphlet printed by England's Society for Psychical Research, published in the mid-eighties, in which professional researcher Frank Podmore wrote of having investigated the reality of ghosts by setting up a committee on haunted houses, and of having exposed numerous cases of fraud among mediums. No specifics as to how the frauds were perpetrated were included, however.

The most useful tract was the report of the Seybert Commission. Published in 1887, this detailed the findings of a three-year investigation of several respected spiritualist mediums by members of the faculty at the University of Pennsylvania. In every case examined, fraud or suspected fraud was uncovered in the presentation of allegedly visible, audible, and tangible evidence of the existence of spirits.

Slate writing, for instance—one of the most common ploys, in which two slates are fastened together so that the writing surfaces face each other and a small pencil between them is made to produce "spirit writing"—was said to be performed "in a manner so closely resembling fraud as to be indistinguishable from it." Other gimmicks such as spirit rappings, movement of objects, and spirit photography were also treated with skepticism. The report's appendices described how spiritualist mediums operated, but here, too, the information was sketchy. There were few details explaining the methods used by mediums to perform their various marvels.

It was nearly four thirty by the time Sabina finished her researches. She returned to the agency to determine if there was any new business to be dealt with before calling it a day. A second wire had been delivered, this one from the Pinkerton office in Washington, which stated essentially the same as the previous response from the Chicago office: they had no file or knowledge of Professor A. Vargas, Annabelle, or the Unified College of the Attuned Impulses. There was also a message from Madame Louella in her spidery hand, typically brief and typically mercenary: *Subject unknown. Word out. Two dollars, dearie.*

Sabina was straightening her desk, preparatory to closing up again, when the telephone bell set up its clamor. The identity of the caller was something of a surprise.

"Mrs. Carpenter?" the gruff male voice said, and when she confirmed it, "Boggs here. Recognize the name?"

Of course she did. Mr. Boggs (she had never been told his first name) was head of the Secret Service's San Francisco field office in the U.S. Mint, and John's superior in the days when John had been the Service's best operative. Boggs had been one of the thirty detectives brought together to form the Service in 1865, and was a personal friend of William P. Wood, its first chief, who had handpicked him for his position here. She had met him only once, a large, graying man with a brusque manner and a penchant for cigars, but John had a great deal of respect for him—more than for any man he had ever known except his father.

"An unexpected pleasure, Mr. Boggs," she said.

"I wish it were. Is your partner available?"

"I'm afraid not, sir. He is out of town."

A noise came over the wire that might have been a bitten-back oath. "When do you expect him back? Soon?"

"By the end of the week, I hope, though it depends on how his investigation progresses."

"Where is he? Can he be reached by telephone?"

"I don't believe so. He left Sunday for Jamestown in the southern Mother Lode, on a job for the Sierra Railway. Is there anything I can help you with, Mr. Boggs?"

There was a long, staticky pause before he said, "The name Long Nick Darrow mean anything to you, Mrs. Carpenter?"

"Long Nick Darrow. Yes, a notorious counterfeiter. John told me of his encounter with the man several years ago."

"Ten, to be exact. Have you heard anything of Darrow recently?"

"No, sir. He's dead, isn't he?"

"So we've presumed," Mr. Boggs said. "What is the name of the man who hired John for Sierra Railway?"

"C. W. Cromarty, the line's division superintendent."

"Based in Jamestown, you said?"

"Yes."

"I'll try contacting John by wire. It's urgent that I speak with him as soon as possible."

"Can you tell me why, Mr. Boggs?"

"Not on the telephone. But it's nothing for you to be concerned about. If you should hear from him before I make contact, inform him of our conversation and ask him to get in touch with me immediately."

The urgent matter might not be cause for concern, Sabina

thought after Boggs ended the call, but it was puzzling and a bit disconcerting nonetheless. According to John, Long Nick Darrow had been one of the slipperiest coney men west of the Mississippi, whom John had tracked down in Seattle and who had died as a result of a pitched battle between them. In his estimation, no koniaker had ever done a better or more distinctive job of bleaching and bill-splitting than Darrow.

The process, he'd explained to her, was one in which a one-dollar note was sliced lengthwise down the center, the two thin sheets then bleached to transparency with chemicals; colored silk threads were placed in the zone systems between the layers to resemble the authentic variety, then the halves were pasted back together, and each side was reprinted from bogus hundred-dollar plates. When done with skill, the counterfeit could be detected only by looking for two giveaways through a magnifying glass: a slight thickness from the paste; and the pressure marks from the original scroll work on the one-dollar bills, marks that couldn't be bleached out along with the colors.

And now, fantastic as it seemed, Long Nick Darrow might not be dead after all. If not, was he back in the counterfeiting business after a long absence, or had he never left it and somehow managed to escape detection the past ten years? Something along these lines must be the reason for Mr. Boggs's apparent apprehension. But why did he want to confer with John? Was it because Darrow was now thought to be in San Francisco or the Bay Area?

Now even more than before, Sabina hoped for her partner's early return from Jamestown.

6

QUINCANNON

Dr. Amos Goodfellow—his full name was lettered on a small sign tacked to his office door—had evidently not yet returned from his ministrations at the Rappahanock mine when Quincannon sought him out at nine o'clock Tuesday morning. The door was locked, and several knuckle raps produced no response.

The dry-goods store downstairs was open for business. He asked the middle-aged, sour-faced clerk if Doc Goodfellow had treated anyone for a severe gash or cut on the hand, wrist, or forearm in the past three days. The clerk either didn't know or refused to say. His only comment was, "Doc treated plenty of cuts and gashes up at the Rappahanock yesterday, I'll wager. Broken bones and worse, too."

Quincannon saw no point in asking his question of any of the other citizens abroad this morning, cooperation being at a minimum in Tuttletown's closed environment. The only person who could answer it was Amos Goodfellow . . . if he turned out not to be as closemouthed as the rest of the locals.

With another unsatisfactory café meal stirring gaseously in his innards, Quincannon rented a horse at the hostelry and rode out Icehouse Road to the field where the breached safe had been abandoned. No one had attempted to move the safe since yesterday, nor come to paw over it so far as he could tell. He examined the box once again, carefully, not expecting to find another useful clue. He didn't, but his peering and probing at the damaged door and hinges did produce a glimmer of an idea as to how the alleged burglarproof safe had been opened.

The morning was warming, the road and meadow completely deserted; except for birdcalls and the distant pound of the stamps, silence prevailed. Quincannon settled himself under the oak tree, gave a satisfactory belch, filled and lighted his briar, and began toying with the idea. Possible, yes, he decided. But he needed more information before he could be even halfway sure.

He rode back to town and once again climbed the outside stairs to Amos Goodfellow's second-floor office. This time he found the door unlocked; the doctor had returned. When he entered, a tall, saturnine man seated at a rolltop desk lifted his head from where it had been resting on folded arms and regarded Quincannon with bleary eyes. He bore a superficial resemblance to Honest Abe and was evidently proud of the fact; the beard he cultivated was decidedly Lincolnesque.

His "Yes?" was followed by a weary, jaw-cracking yawn. "Sorry. I've been up most of the night."

"The Rappahanock mine cave-in."

"That's right. Two men dead, nine injured."

"I'm sorry to hear it."

"Dangerous profession, mining." Goodfellow yawned again. "You look hale and hearty, whoever you are. What can I do for you?"

Quincannon identified himself. Goodfellow had heard of the theft of the safe and its discovery, naturally, but because of the mine cave-in he wasn't aware of Quincannon's mission in Tuttle-town. He seemed less wary of outsiders than most of his fellow citizens, and willing to cooperate when the question of whether he had treated anyone for a severe gash or cut in the past three days was put to him.

"I have, yes," he said. "Two men and a ten-year-old."

"The men were locals, I take it?"

"Yes."

"Who would they be?"

"A railroad section hand named . . . let's see, Jacobsen, I think it was. Consequences of a fall. Gashed his arm and broke his wrist in two places. I had a difficult time setting the bones."

"And the other man, Doctor?"

"One of the Schneider brothers—Bodo. Deep cut on the back of his left hand and wrist."

"Miners? Railroad men?"

"No. The Schneiders own the icehouse."

"Ah. Big fellows, are they? Brawny?"

"Yes, of course. Men who make their living cutting and haul-ing ice can hardly be puny."

"Have they been in Tuttletown long?"

"Not long. They bought the business about three years ago."

"Do you happen to know where they came from?"

"I've been told they owned a similar business down in Bishop," Goodfellow said, "but I don't know for certain. They're a close-mouthed pair."

"Peaceable men, law-abiding?"

"Well, the younger, Jakob, has a reputation for rowdiness when he's had too much to drink. But so do half the men who live and work in these parts."

"Do the Schneiders live at or near their icehouse?"

"No. In a cabin on Table Mountain." The doctor frowned. "Do you suspect them of stealing the safe from the express office?"

"At this point," Quincannon said, "I suspect everyone and no one." Which wasn't quite the truth, but it permitted him to take his leave without further questions.

Having returned his rented horse to the hostler's, he walked to the side street that led to Icehouse Road. A brisk five-minute stroll brought him to the icehouse. He had paid little enough attention to it the times he had passed by yesterday and only slightly more this morning; now he paused at the edge of the road for a closer study while he loaded the last of his tobacco into his briar.

The ivy-covered stone building sat creekside a short distance off the road, connected to it by a graveled lane. Set apart from it on the near side was a shedlike structure with a single facing window, likely the business office. There was no sign of activity there or at a wagon entrance barred by a set of wide double doors at the far end. A somewhat dilapidated wooden livery barn and a rough-fenced corral occupied a grassy section between the road and the creek. No conveyances or animals were visible from where Quincannon stood. Either one or both of the Schneider brothers were out delivering ice, or their wagon and dray horses were tucked up inside the barn.

When he'd seen enough, he walked at a leisurely pace back to Main Street and entered the stone-housed general store near the hotel, Swerer's by name. As he paid for his purchases, the garrulous young fellow behind the counter took pride in informing him that the writer Bret Harte had once clerked there. Quincannon was more impressed by the outlandish prices charged for one small dark lantern, one tin of lamp oil, and a plug of shag-cut tobacco. Not that the outlay bothered him; these amounts, along with the price of the horse rental and other expenses, would be added to the bill he would present to the Sierra Railway Company for services rendered.

He took the lantern and lamp oil to the hotel and stored them in his room. Then he went to the railroad depot. C. W. Cromarty's private car, he was pleased to see, still sat on the siding onto which it had been shunted the day before.

"Well, Mr. Quincannon?" Cromarty said. He was alone in the car, seated at a desk almost as cluttered with papers as the one in his Jimtown office. "Have you come to report progress in your investigation?"

"Not exactly, though progress has been made. Do you intend spending another night here in Tuttletown?"

"Not unless there is good cause." He removed a lighted cheroot from one corner of his mouth, though not in time to prevent an inch of ash from spilling onto the front of his vest. "Is there?"

"There may well be. Unless you have pressing business in Jamestown, I suggest you lay over until tomorrow morning."

"Why? Do you expect to have finished your investigation by then?"

"Perhaps, if all goes well."

"Does that mean you know how the safe was breached?"

"Perhaps."

"And who stole it? And where the gold is?"

"Perhaps."

Cromarty aimed the cheroot at Quincannon as if it were a pistol. "Dammit, man, don't be evasive. If you know the answers to this confounded mystery, let me hear them."

"Not until I'm certain. You're paying me for definite results, corroborated facts, not premature speculation."

"You expect to have those results by morning?"

"I do. One way or another. Either the matter will be resolved by then, or I'll need more time to explore other possibilities. Will you be staying over, Mr. Cromarty? Or shall I report to you in Jamestown tomorrow?"

The division superintendent restored the cheroot to his mouth, bit down hard on the end of it. "You leave me little choice in the matter," he said. "Adam Newell and I have no urgent need to return to Jamestown. I'll be here in the morning."

Quincannon spent the remainder of the day in what amounted to a waiting mode. He asked as many Tuttletown residents as deigned to be responsive discreet questions about the Schneider brothers, learning little more than what Doc Goodfellow had told him; they were not well liked, the prices they charged for blocks and bags of ice being considered exorbitant, and so evidently made a less than comfortable living from their business. Yet another poor dinner at the Miners Rest Café and unproductive visits to a trio of saloons occupied his time until an hour past nightfall.

Once more in his room at Cremer House, he stripped to his long johns and again made an effort to settle himself on the mound of bricks disguised as a mattress. He set his internal clock, a mechanism so unfailing that he never had cause to use one of the alarm variety. He was asleep within minutes, this time without the aid of a temperance tract.

7

QUINCANNON

At three A.M., dressed in layers of clothing and his buttoned-up Chesterfield, Quincannon slipped out of the hotel's side entrance. In one gloved hand he carried the dark lantern, its wick already lit and the shutter tightly closed. A thickening layer of clouds deepened the night's blackness, which suited his purpose well. The few scattered night-lights in business establishments along Main Street, pale by contrast, were oil lamps with their wicks turned down low; electric lights had been installed in Jamestown, but not here as yet.

Main Street was all but deserted at this hour; even the saloons had closed. He avoided the one man he saw, a lurching individual obviously under the influence of strong drink, as he made his way through the town to the side street that led to Icehouse Road. Here he had the night to himself. The darkness was unbroken except for distant flickers of lamplight that marked the locations of the mines and cabins at the higher elevations.

The road in both directions was deserted when he neared the icehouse. He veered over to the tall cottonwoods that bordered it on the south. Under the trees and along the nearby creek, the shadows were as black as India ink. The stone building was likewise shrouded, as were the shedlike office, the livery barn and corral. He stood listening for half a minute. A night bird's cry, a faint sound from the direction of the corral that was likely the restless movement of a horse. Otherwise, silence. Even the mine stamps were temporarily still.

Quincannon picked his way through dew-wet grass to the rear entrance to the icehouse. Naturally, the pair of heavy wooden doors were secure. He opened the lantern's shutter a crack, shielding the light with his body, and quickly examined the iron hasp and padlock. Well and good. The padlock was large and looked new, but it was of inferior manufacture.

He closed the shutter, set the lantern down. The set of lock picks he carried, an unintentional gift from a burglar he'd once snaffled, were the best ill-gotten funds could fabricate, and long practice had taught him how to manipulate them as dexterously as any housebreaker. The absence of light hampered his efforts here; it took him three times longer, working by feel, than it would have under normal circumstances to free the padlock's staple. Not a sound disturbed the stillness the entire time.

He removed the lock, hung it from the hasp, and opened one door half just wide enough to ease his body through. The temperature inside was several degrees colder. When he opened the lantern's shutter all the way, he saw that he was in a narrow space that sloped downward and was blocked on the inner side by a second set of doors. These, fortunately, were not locked.

The interior of the icehouse was colder still, as frigid as a ward politician's heart. Quincannon opened the lantern's eye to its fullest, shined the light around.

This was an old-fashioned ice-harvesting business, without benefit of an expensive modern compression refrigeration unit. The stone walls, he judged, were at least two feet thick and the wooden floor set six feet or so below ground level. Large and small blocks of ice lined both walls, cut from the creek or more likely from the Stanislaus River during the winter months. Thick layers of straw covered the floor, and more was packed around the ice blocks; the low ceiling would likewise be insulated with straw to help keep the sun's heat from penetrating. A trapdoor in the middle of the floor doubtless gave access to a stone- or brick-walled pit that would also be ice-filled, a solid mass ready to be broken by ax and chisel into smaller chunks as needed.

He played the light beam around more slowly, looking for a likely hiding place. None presented itself. The cold had begun to penetrate his clothing, to numb fingertips inside the fleece-lined gloves; he hurried to the far end and began his search, stamping his feet to maintain circulation.

By the time he had covered three-quarters of the space, finding nothing but ice and straw, he was chilled to the marrow. But the high good humor with which he had embarked on this nocturnal quest remained intact; so did his confidence. The Schneider brothers had committed the robbery and the stolen gold was hidden somewhere in here. Logic dictated that it couldn't be anywhere else.

A few minutes later, his faith in his deductions was amply rewarded.

At the base of one wall not far from the entrance, he uncovered a cavelike space formed by ice blocks and a thick pile of straw. The bullion and sacks of dust were piled under the straw—the entire booty, from the look of it.

A satisfied smile creased his pirate's beard. He pocketed one of the sacks, heaped straw over the rest of the gold. Quickly, then, he made his exit from the building, with the intention of replacing the padlock and then hastening back into town to locate Constable Teague.

The intention, however, was thwarted. No sooner had he stepped outside than something like an angry hornet whizzed past him, smacked into the wall, and dislodged a stone chip that stung his cheek.

Quincannon had been fired upon often enough in his professional career to react instantly and instinctively. All in one motion he dropped the lantern, pulled his head in, and threw himself forward and down as the crack of the shot split the night. He struck the ground flat on his belly, slid through the wet grass. He was turning onto his side, tearing the Chesterfield open and groping within to free the Navy Colt from its holster, when the second slug came humming by. Wherever it hit was nowhere near him.

This time he spied the muzzle flash. The shooter was over by the barn some forty yards away, his weapon evidently a handgun. But the absence of any kind of moonlight or starlight made it difficult to distinguish shapes among the clotted shadows;

Quincannon couldn't tell if the man had moved or was still in the same place.

One of the Schneider brothers, no doubt. Damn and damnation! What had drawn him here in the middle of the night? And the other one . . . was he present, too?

Quincannon had the Navy out now. With his teeth, he pulled the glove off his right hand and took a tight grip on the weapon. Then he lay motionless, the dark night his ally; Schneider couldn't see him any better than he could see Schneider. But the man still had an advantage: the barn was closer to the road than Quincannon's position before the icehouse. To attempt an escape in that direction would be folly.

Lie here and wait to see if Schneider came to investigate his marksmanship? No. Not without knowing if the man had a lantern of his own, or if his brother was somewhere nearby, possibly sneaking around behind the icehouse. The creek, then? It ran between banks five or six feet high, the near bank some twenty yards from where he lay; if he could get down into the cut, he ought to be able to make his way back toward town unseen. The grass was tall enough to cover a squirming crawl to it as long as he was quiet about it.

He began moving, slowly at first, propelling himself with his free hand. Fear was a stranger to him, but he could feel a thin ooze of sweat on his brow despite the cold and the dampness. A short distance from the bank, his extended hand struck and loosened something smallish and solid. The noise the bump and roll made seemed loud in his ears, froze him into immobility. But the sound must not have carried, for no third shot came, nor did any movement from the direction of the barn break the heavy silence.

Quincannon resumed his crawl. The bank's edge was all but invisible; it was the gurgling murmur of creek water close below that told him when he'd reached it. But he had no way of knowing how steep it was until he wiggled forward, twisted his body, and commenced a sliding descent. It was not strictly vertical, fortunately, but still steep enough so that he had to clutch at vines of ivy and clumps of fern to keep from tumbling into the stream. The slithering sounds his body made were muted by the water's quick-running passage.

Near the bottom, a section of brush and root-tangled earth ended his slide. He dug one boot heel into the bank; the other foot slipped into the icy water before he could brace himself. He yanked it out and managed to shove himself erect, the brush tearing at his coat. And he bit back a sharp oath when he attempted to step gingerly into the creek.

The water was only ankle-deep, but the rocks in the streambed were not pebbles; most were large, the size of baseballs, and packed loosely together. Walking on them in daylight would have been difficult enough; in the inky dark you couldn't see where you were putting your feet. Even moving at a retarded pace would be risking a fall, serious injury.

A mistake, coming down here, he thought grimly. He might well have trapped himself.

But there was still a chance if the bank remained slanted and not too overgrown ahead, so that he could ease along it far enough and silently enough to get past the icehouse. Then he could crawl out, make his escape. *If* the Schneider brother by the barn hadn't realized where he'd gone and didn't come hunting him meanwhile. And *if* the other Schneider brother wasn't hidden, waiting, somewhere near the icehouse.

Two hands were necessary to feel his way along the bank; that meant holstering the Navy. Best to do that anyway, for if he tripped or fell, the weapon might be jarred out of his hand and lost in the darkness. More brush, roots, vines, clumps of fern impeded his progress, and more than once one foot or the other slid into the water, chilling him even more. Every few feet he paused to strain his ears. Still nothing to hear but the voice of the creek and the thin, labored plaint of his breathing.

He'd gone an indeterminate distance when light suddenly flashed on the flat above. It arced, bobbing this way and that— Schneider, with a lantern of his own or the one Quincannon had carried, searching for him.

Quincannon attempted to increase his speed, only to come upon a mass of something that blocked his way. One groping hand touched a cold surface just in time to prevent him from falling over whatever it was, but not in time to avoid kicking a loose stone that clattered metallically against its surface— surely a carrying sound. Cursing under his breath, he stood motionless, head tilted upward. The light still sliced the darkness above, but in the same dancing arc rather than steadying toward where he was. Schneider was too far away to have heard the noise.

The obstruction on the bank was mounded earth split by something thick and thigh-high that extended at a downward angle into the creek. Quincannon ran his ungloved hand over its ridged surface, identified it: a section of drainpipe some three feet in diameter and covered with stalks of ivy. *Hell, damn, and blast!* In order to get over and around it he would have to risk stepping into the treacherous stream. And for all he knew, there was more obstruction on the far side.

One other choice: climb out here, on the hope that the light wouldn't pick him out before he could pinpoint Schneider's location. The fact that only the single beam swept the grassy flat, and that there was still nothing to hear, indicated that the man was alone up there. Just the one brother and himself in this tense duel.

The cutbank here was not quite as steep as it had been farther down. Ivy grew thickly here; using the thick stalks, Quincannon was able to pull himself upward with relative ease. Partway to the top he thought he heard something, halted to listen again.

Swishing, sliding sounds above and not far away: stealthy footfalls in the wet grass.

In the next second the light steadied. He couldn't be certain, but it seemed to be pointed off to his left.

He moved just enough to draw the Navy again. The sounds above continued, the light holding steady; it was difficult to tell in the darkness, but Schneider seemed to be moving at an angle to his left. Quickly, then, Quincannon eeled his body the rest of the way up, left hand clinging to the ivy and knees digging into the soft earth.

As soon as his head cleared the top edge, he spied Schneider less than fifteen feet away, creeping forward now in a half crouch, the shape of the weapon extended in his right hand visible in the lantern's glow. Not heading in Quincannon's direction but straight ahead to the cutbank, which meant he was looking that way, too.

Quincannon braced himself, took a firm grip on his right wrist with his left, and drew a bead. And when Schneider paused near the bank, he squeezed off three rounds in rapid succession.

Shooting in the dark was tricky business, even at relatively close range and with the lantern outlining his quarry, but he prided himself on his marksmanship even under such adverse conditions as these. One and possibly two bullets struck Schneider, brought forth a surprised outcry and knocked him off his pins. The lantern, popped loose from his grasp, had bounced to one side and remained burning at an angle that revealed Schneider where he lay.

The wound was not a mortal one—Quincannon could see him thrashing around in the grass, hear him moaning—but it was incapacitating enough to keep him down with no attempt to rise up and return fire. Long seconds passed before Quincannon was sure that Schneider wasn't shamming, then he levered himself up over the rim and onto his feet. The Navy at arm's length, he cautiously approached the fallen man.

Schneider lay on his back, still thrashing, though more feebly now. His moans ceased when Quincannon snapped out, "Raise up with your weapon, Schneider, and you're a dead man."

"I ain't got it no more, I dropped it." The gruff Teutonic voice was thick with pain.

"That better not be a lie. Where are you hit?"

"Arm, hip. Shattered a bone, damn you, I can't feel my leg."

Quincannon moved close enough to determine that both hands were visible and empty. Then he sidestepped to where the lantern lay, picked it up, shined the beam on Schneider. He was a big one, to be sure, at least fifty pounds over two hundred. His bearded face contorted into a squinting grimace and long straggly hair glistened blackly in the light.

"Where's your brother?"

"Home. I come down here alone."

"Why, at this hour?"

No response.

"Worried about the gold, is that it? Arrived just in time to see me breaking into the icehouse."

"Goddamn flycop. How'd you know Bodo and me stole it, where we had it hid?"

"Never mind that. You'll find out soon enough."

A grunt, another moan. "*Gott im Himmel,* man, get me the doctor before I bleed to death."

Quincannon hunted around until he found Schneider's dropped sidearm, a large-caliber Colt. He slid it into the pocket of his mud-caked Chesterfield. He had no qualms about leaving the wounded man here in the wet grass; criminals, especially those who would have had no qualms about putting a lethal bullet in *him,* deserved to suffer for their sins.

With the lantern guiding him, he hurried to the road and back to town—to fetch Constable Teague, first, and then Dr. Amos Goodfellow.

8

QUINCANNON

At a few minutes past nine on Wednesday morning, in C. W. Cromarty's private car, Quincannon prepared to hold court.

Once the wounded Schneider, Jakob by given name, had been tended to and removed to a cell in the Tuttletown jail, Teague had deputized a group of citizens that included the express agent, Booker, and thence proceeded to the brothers' Table Mountain cabin. Bodo Schneider had been arrested without incident, and was now ensconsed in a cell adjoining Jakob's. Quincannon, meanwhile, had awakened Cromarty and his chief engineer to report the good news. The gold subsequently had been removed from the icehouse and turned over to Booker for safekeeping.

Over the objections of Teague, Cromarty, and Newell, Quincannon had withheld explanation of how the burglarproof safe had been successfully burgled until all these worthies could be assembled together. He admitted to a dramatic streak in his nature; if he hadn't become a detective, he might have gone on the stage and become a notable dramatic actor. "Ham, you mean," Sabina had said when he mentioned this to her once, but he'd forgiven her.

Cromarty had been effusive in his praise initially, but he had grown impatient in the interim. Now he said, "You've done a splendid job, Mr. Quincannon, and there's no gainsaying that you're something of a wizard to have solved the riddle in less than twenty-four hours, but—"

"I prefer the term 'artist,'" Quincannon interrupted. Humility was not one of his virtues, if in fact it was a virtue. "You might even say I am the Rembrandt of crime solvers."

Teague said, "Who's Rembrandt?" but no one answered him.

"Be that as it may," Cromarty said, "there is no need to keep us in suspense any longer. How did you deduce the identity of the thieves and the location of the gold?"

"Yes, and how did they get the safe open? That's what I'd most like to know."

The two railroad men nodded emphatic agreement.

Quincannon took his time loading and lighting his briar. When he had it drawing to his satisfaction, he fluffed his beard and said, "Very well, gentlemen, I'll begin by noting the clues that led me to the solution. When I examined the abandoned safe I found several items of interest. To begin with, the bloodstains. Obviously one of the thieves had suffered a wound that bled copiously during the robbery, one severe enough to bleed again when the empty safe was transported the following day. Naturally such a wound would require medical attention. Amos Goodfellow being the only doctor in Tuttletown, I consulted with him and learned that he had treated Bodo Schneider for a deep cut on his hand and wrist. That, and the doctor's description of the two brothers as brawny fellows, pointed me in their direction."

Newell asked, "And the other items of interest in the abandoned safe?"

"The fact that the interior was cold and damp, too cold and damp for the night and morning air to have been responsible. A hard residue of putty where the chisel marks were located on the door. And a piece of straw caught on one of the bolts. Straw, as of course you all know, is used to pack blocks and chunks of ice to preserve them by slowing the melting process."

"Seems like pretty flimsy evidence," Teague observed. "And what's putty got to do with it?"

Quincannon addressed the constable's statement, ignoring his question for the moment. "On the contrary, the evidence was not at all flimsy when taken in toto and combined with the location of the discarded safe—less than a mile from the icehouse. The thieves saw no need and had no desire, given Bodo Schneider's wounded hand and the cumbersome weight of the safe, to transport it any further than that meadow. They were foolishly certain no one would suspect them of the crime."

"How did you know the gold was hidden in the icehouse?" Cromarty asked. "The Schneiders might just as well have secreted it elsewhere."

"Might have, yes, but it would have required additional risk. The weight of the gold and the necessity of finding a different hiding place also argued against it having been moved any appreciable distance. As far as they were concerned, it was perfectly secure inside the icehouse until it could be disposed of piecemeal."

"Are you saying that the icehouse was where the safe was opened?"

"I am. It's the only place it could have been managed in this region at this time of year." Quincannon puffed out a cumulus of smoke, shifted his gaze to Teague. "Do you recall my stating yesterday that the *how* and the *why* of the crime were linked?"

"I do."

"And so they are. Once I determined that the Schneiders must be guilty, it was a simple matter of cognitive reasoning to deduce the *how*."

"Fancy talk," Teague said. "Say it in plain English, man. How'd they bust into that safe?"

"Strictly speaking, they didn't. The safe was opened from the inside, not the outside."

"From the *inside*? What the devil are you talking about?"

"The application of a simple law of physics," Quincannon said. "After the safe had been allowed to chill inside the ice-house, the Schneiders turned it on its back and hammered a wedge into the crack of the door along the bottom edge, the purpose being to widen the crack through to the inside—a procedure similar in nature to their objective with the express-office door. Then, using a bucket and a funnel, they poured water into the safe until it was full. The final steps were to seal the crack with hard-drying putty"—he glanced meaningfully at the constable as he spoke—"and then to pack ice around the safe and cover the whole with straw."

Newell smacked his forehead with the heel of his hand. "Of

course! The object being to freeze the water inside. Water expands as much as one-seventh of its volume when it freezes."

"Exactly. Once the water in the safe froze, the intense pressure from the ice caused the door's hinges to rupture. It was a simple matter, then, for the pair to chip out the ice and remove the gold. The residue in the safe melted after they carted it away to the field, hence the cold, damp interior."

Cromarty, Newell, even Teague were satisfied. And Quincannon was well pleased with himself, for once again he had solved the seemingly insoluable by a combination of observation and deductive reasoning—qualities which made him the most accomplished detective west of the Mississippi River, if not in the entire nation. Anyone who didn't agree with that assessment—other than Sabina, whose own talents he respected and for whom he made allowances—was a dunderhead.

Marshal Samuel B. Halloran of Jamestown, for instance.

Quincannon chuckled to himself. Halloran, all unwittingly, had provided him with one other minor clue to the solution of this investigation, one he hadn't seen fit to mention in his summation. He was saving it to use as part of his gloat when he sought out that dunderhead lawman before departing the Queen of the Mines.

"You may be a fancy-pants detective in San Francisco," Halloran had said in Cromarty's office, "but you don't cut no ice up here." Ah, but he had—figuratively if not literally.

He'd cut more ice in Tuttletown last night, by godfrey, than the Schneiders had from inside that so-called burglarproof safe!

The private car, once more coupled to a Baldwin locomotive, departed Tuttletown a short while later for the return trip to Jamestown. The only passengers were Quincannon and Cromarty, Newell having additional business to attend to at the railroad construction site near the Stanislaus River.

The division superintendent, busy at his desk as they chuffed along the edge of the valley toward Table Mountain, was disinclined to conversation, which suited Quincannon. He'd had no sleep since leaving the Cremer Hotel at three A.M., and his tense skirmish with Jakob Schneider and the night's and morning's other events had taken their toll. Settled comfortably in one of the tufted chairs, he was thinking of Sabina in a pleasant near doze when a sudden exclamation from Cromarty roused him.

"I have something here for you, Mr. Quincannon."

He turned in his chair. "Yes?"

"A wire that came for you in Jamestown and was delivered to me earlier. I completely forgot about it in all the excitement; came upon it just now in my coat pocket."

Quincannon felt a faint stirring of alarm. The wire must be from Sabina; no one else knew he'd come to the southern Mother Lode. And she wouldn't have wired him unless some sort of emergency had come up. He snatched the envelope out of Cromarty's extended hand, tore it open.

No, it wasn't from Sabina. But his relief was short-lived, consumed by surprise and puzzlement as he read the message.

> URGENT I SEE YOU SOONEST STOP
> PRINCIPAL IN SEATTLE MATTER TEN YEARS
> AGO APPARENTLY NOT DECEASED STOP

BELIEVED IN BUSINESS AGAIN HERE STOP
WIRE REPLY WITH TIME OF EXPECTED
RETURN TO CITY STOP
                    BOGGS

Crusty old Boggs, his superior during his San Francisco ten-ure as an operative of the Secret Service. Quincannon retained a soft spot for the man; Boggs had taught him a great deal about investigative work, and been a staunch friend during the darkest period of his life. Press of their now separate careers prevented them from seeing much of each other these days, and this was the first time Boggs had sought his assistance since he'd left the Service.

"The Seattle matter" referred to a case involving a counter-feiter named Long Nick Darrow. Quincannon sat frowning, working his memory. He recalled following a circuitous trail of counterfeit hundred-dollar bills north through Oregon to Wash-ington State and finally to a warehouse near Colman Wharf on the Seattle waterfront where the coney man was manufacturing his queer. During a nocturnal raid by him and agents from the Seattle branch, a lamp had been knocked over and the tinder-dry warehouse set ablaze.

Darrow had managed to escape, with Quincannon in close pursuit. The chase had ended in a fierce hand-to-hand struggle between them on a deserted pier nearby. He had deflected a knife thrust that sent the blade plunging into Darrow's torso in-stead of his own. Darrow had staggered away, plunged into the black waters of the harbor. The fact that his body had not been found, nor had there been any word of him in the years since, seemed to bear out the presumption that the blackleg had met his Maker that night.

Yet according to this wire, Darrow might have somehow managed to survive both the knife wound and the icy harbor water, and was now not only back at his old trade but plying it in or near San Francisco. It seemed fantastic. A counterfeiter whose work resembled his must be responsible. If Darrow was alive, where had he been the past ten years? Certainly not somewhere working at his old trade with a new set of plates, the originals having been destroyed in the fire along with the engraver who made them, else his distinctive product would have come to light before now. Counterfeiters, no matter how practiced or clever, had never outwitted the Secret Service for long during Quincannon's tenure, and hadn't since, he'd wager.

What was also puzzling about Boggs's wire was the urgent need to consult with his former operative. The sector chief had a handful of well-trained agents on staff and could call on as many others as might be needed, and the fact that Quincannon had handled the original case was of no real consequence. Nor could it be to rehash the events of that flaming night on the Seattle waterfront; Quincannon had recorded them all in detail in his written and verbal reports. There must be some other reason for Boggs's request.

Well, there was nothing to be gained by speculating now on what it might be. He would meet with Boggs as soon as he returned to the city and find out then—late tomorrow afternoon, if he could book passage out of Jamestown early enough today and if the trains from there and Stockton ran on time, always a problematical circumstance.

Home tomorrow, at any rate, which fact he would wire to Boggs as soon as they arrived in Jimtown. And to Sabina as well, along with brief preliminary word of his success in Tuttletown.

9

SABINA

Sabina's second audience with Professor A. Vargas on Thursday afternoon and third on Friday morning followed along similar lines as the first. At Thursday's he professed to have made contact with his spirit control, and that Angkar had agreed to seek out the shade of the mythical Gregory Milford; at the just completed Friday sitting, he claimed that Angkar had made contact with Gregory, who was "quite happy in the Afterworld though still adjusting to spirit life." It was possible that communication might be established between brother and sister at Saturday's séance, he said, though Angkar had told him that the alleged "malevolent forces" were particularly active at present. It was therefore necessary that her "psychic energy be properly focused" at the séance in order to circumvent the evil influence. Which, of course, required the third audience and another ten-dollar "donation."

At both the second and third, Vargas probed for additional

information about the Milford family's finances, and for personal details about Gregory's life and activities before "his passage beyond the veil." And deflected Sabina's attempts to question him about his and the college's past activities and the reason for his move to San Francisco as neatly as she deflected his subtle attempts at seduction. The remainder of each session was taken up with embellishments in his line of double-talk about attuned impulses, paranormal rapport, spatial and temporal laws, and theocratic unity.

There was no doubt that Vargas was an out-and-out fraud and a shameless womanizer to boot. The answer to Sabina's wire to the Pinkerton Agency's New York office provided evidence of both facts.

Six years previously, one Abraham Vargas had acted as assistant to a fraudulent clairvoyant known as the "Albany Seer" who had bilked gullible *Social Register* clients of thousands of dollars before being unmasked and arrested. Vargas had been charged, tried, and convicted along with him, receiving a six-month prison sentence. And during the trial, it had come to light that both men had indulged in immoral escapades with more than one of their female acolytes.

Nothing was known in New York of Vargas since his release. But he had obviously learned enough tricks from his employer to set up his own fake spiritualist confidence game. Where he had operated the Unified College of the Attuned Impulses before traveling west was anyone's guess. As was where and how he had acquired the services of the cold-eyed Annabelle; there was no record of her having been involved with Vargas or the "Albany Seer" in New York. Another of his sexual conquests, no doubt.

Winthrop Buckley would surely be as satisfied as Sabina that the professor was a fraud, but an ardent occultist such as Mrs. Buckley might well be inclined to give Vargas the benefit of the doubt unless she was presented with empirical proof of his duplicity. This, Sabina felt sure, could be accomplished at Saturday's séance, assuming Vargas's bag of mediumistic tricks was as standard as she expected it must be from her client's description of what had transpired the previous Saturday.

The task of providing that proof would be made even easier if she had a better idea of how those tricks were worked. And if she could talk John into attending the séance with her.

His wire from Jamestown had arrived just before close of business on Thursday, letting her know that he had successfully wrapped up his investigation for the Sierra Railway Company and expected to be back in the city sometime this afternoon. Both bits of news had pleased her, the latter more than the former. And not only because she coveted his assistance.

The old adage was true where John was concerned: absence did indeed make the heart grow fonder.

The narrow storefront where Madame Louella conducted her Gypsy fortune-telling dodge was on Kearney near Pine, sandwiched between the shop of a woman who made what she billed as "fashionable cloaks for the ladies" and a grifter who called himself the "Napoleon of Necromancers." A large sign above the entrance proclaimed that Madame Louella SEES ALL, KNOWS ALL, TELLS ALL and would inform those who wished to know what their futures held for the price of twenty-five cents per reading.

Sabina climbed a short flight of stairs to the second floor and entered to the tinkling of a bell. The anteroom was empty, but the low murmur of voices from behind the drawn black curtain that separated it from Madame Louella's inner sanctum indicated a visitor. The odor of incense permeated the room, a different variety than that used by A. Vargas but no less unpleasant. Black curtains, cabalistic signs, incense—all seemed de rigueur with those who practiced spiritualism, fortune-telling, mind reading, and other such flimflams.

She sat on one of three wooden chairs to wait. The incense seemed particularly strong today; if she hadn't stopped at a tea shop for lunch on her way to Kearney Street, the biting odor would have had an even queasier effect on her stomach than it did. It was one reason Sabina avoided coming here except when absolutely necessary. The other was that a little of Madame Louella in person went a long way. Absence in the fortune-teller's case did *not* make the heart grow fonder.

Her wait, fortunately, was not long. The curtain was soon drawn aside and a corpulent man wearing a satisfied smile emerged. He smiled at Sabina, bowed slightly, set a large derby firmly atop his bald head, and exited. Once the bell ceased tinkling, Madame Louella's turbaned head appeared, then the rest of her large body encased as usual in a robe of tarnished-gold color emblazoned with mystic symbols in black and crimson. The turban was also gold, a fat blue costume jewel set into the middle of it. Stray black curls straggled from beneath the cloth.

When she saw Sabina, her solemn expression dissolved into a bright-eyed smile. "Well, hello there, dearie. What brings you here this fine afternoon? Come to pay the two dollars you owe me, eh?"

"Those, and perhaps a few more."

"So? I've yet to uncover any information on Professor Vargas and the Unified College of the Attuned Impulses. He hasn't been operating in the city long and has done nothing to attract attention." In the grifters' community, she meant.

Sabina said, "There is another way you can earn an additional fee."

"How large an additional fee?"

"That remains to be determined. Large enough to suit you, I should think."

The woman's nostrils twitched visibly. To her, the whiff of money to be had was stronger than that of any other odor including her dratted incense. As a prod, she commenced her usual litany of complaints: how dreadful business had been of late, how her rent was in arrears and she was living hand to mouth, how her lot in life was an affront to a woman born with Romany blood in her veins and the gift of foretelling the future.

"Romany blood, my foot," Sabina said affably. "You're as much a Gypsy as I am, you old fraud."

Madame Louella cackled. "True enough," she admitted. "But business really has been poor lately. Both kinds," she added meaningfully.

Nonsense. The woman made enough gathering and selling information to pay her bills and keep her in relative comfort. But Sabina refrained from stating the fact, saying instead, "Be candid with me, and your primary source of income will soon improve."

"I'm always willing to be candid for the right price, dearie."

Louella led the way through the curtain into her "fortune room," one not unlike Vargas's private office—another similarity in the trappings utilized by paranormal tricksters. Walls painted black, window black-curtained to keep out light, a table draped in black cloth and two facing chairs. And the only illumination an enormous crystal globe treated with a phosphorescent chemical that gave it an eerie inner glow—the same sort of trick A. Vargas used to light the table in his consulting room.

She lowered her bulk onto her pillowed chair, waited for Sabina to be seated, then said, "Now, then. What's your proposition?"

"I assume you're familiar with the methods used by fake mediums to perform their séance tricks—ghostly manifestations, table-tipping, slate writing, and the like. True?"

"Perhaps," the old fraud said slyly. "You're wanting me to spill trade secrets, eh? In order to put this fake medium Vargas out of commission, I suppose?"

"Do you object?"

"Why should I object? He's competition, ain't he? How much will you pay?"

"That depends on how much you reveal."

Louella pretended to consider. "Twenty dollars is a nice round sum."

"So is five dollars."

"For all I know? Pshaw!"

"Ten, then."

"That'll buy you half."

They haggled back and forth, finally settling on fifteen dollars.

John would have considered the price exorbitant, despite the fact that the outlay would be added to Winthrop Buckley's bill, but Sabina had expected to pay a heftier-than-usual sum to obtain the details she sought.

And obtain them she did. Even John would have to admit that the half hour she spent in the company of Madame Louella was worth the time and expense.

It was one thirty when Sabina left the fortune-teller. She had arranged a two o'clock meeting with Winthrop Buckley at his office, to give him both a written and a verbal report on her findings and to inform him of her plans for Saturday night. The distance from Kearney Street to the Montgomery Block being relatively short and the weather still balmy, she once again made passage by what John referred to as shank's mare.

As expected, Mr. Buckley was satisfied with her conclusions about Vargas and the Unified College of the Attuned Impulses—"I knew he would turn out to be a damned . . . excuse me, a blasted phony"—and in agreement that it would take incontestable evidence to convince his wife. "How do you intend to go about providing it, Mrs. Carpenter?"

"By revealing to everyone present at the séance that his spirit-world manifestations are nothing more than parlor tricks."

"You're certain you can accomplish that? That you know how the tricks are done?"

"Most of those you described, yes."

"Including that business with the rope and its missing knots?"

"Yes."

"Is there anything I can do to help?" Mr. Buckley asked.

"Other than maintaining the pretense of belief in what transpires at the séance, no. I intend to ask my partner, John Quincannon, to attend with me—I've already set the stage for his presence with Vargas. Nothing more is needed."

Buckley sighed. "Poor Margaret. She'll be devastated, but it has to be done. Her obsessive need to speak with our poor daughter . . . unhealthy and futile. Perhaps this will make her realize that the living can't communicate with the dead."

Sabina's response was circumspect. "Not through frauds such as A. Vargas at any rate," she said.

10

SABINA

It was just past four-thirty when John walked into the agency toting his traveling valise. He looked rumpled, weary, and a trifle nonplussed. In answer to her greeting he said cheerfully enough, "Ah, it's good to be back, my dear," and crossed to her desk to bestow a light kiss on her cheek. She responded with a smile.

"Uncomfortable trip?" she asked.

"No more so than the one to Jamestown. But at least the train from Stockton arrived on schedule for a change." A frown ridged his broad brow. "In time for me to make a brief stop before I came here, not that it did me any benefit."

"Mr. Boggs's office at the Mint?"

"Yes. I expected he'd be there, but he wasn't. He wired me, as I'm sure you know, and I sent him a return wire with my travel plans."

"Called away on another matter, probably."

"So he wrote in a message he left for me. He'll be available again in the morning. You had a conversation with him, I take it?"

"He telephoned for you on Wednesday."

"Did he tell you why he wants to see me?"

"Only that it concerns a counterfeiter named Long Nick Darrow."

"A counterfeiter perhaps come back to life after ten years in a watery grave."

"And perhaps active again at his old trade," Sabina said. "Mystifying, if so."

"To say the least."

"Why do you suppose Mr. Boggs would want to involve you in the government's investigation?"

"He gave no hint in his wire. Something to do, I suppose, with the fact that I was the operative who tracked Darrow down and the last known person to see him alive."

"You knew his handiwork well?"

"Yes, but so did Boggs."

"Did Darrow ever operate in the Bay Area?"

"Not to my knowledge," John said. "Always in the Pacific Northwest, specifically Seattle. Yet another puzzle, if he is back in the business of manufacturing and shoving queer."

"Will you assist Mr. Boggs if he requests it?"

"Naturally. I owe him any number of favors."

Sabina couldn't resist asking, "At a request for our usual fee?"

John looked at her askance, though not without a certain wistfulness, and made no reply. He went to sit at his desk, where he produced his pipe and began to load the bowl with black tobacco from his waterproof pouch. Try as she might, she could not convince him to change his dreadful brand to one less odorous.

To make up for her jab at his acquisitive nature, she said, "Tell me about your investigation for Sierra Railway, John. It was successful, I trust?"

That perked him up, as she had known it would. There was nothing her partner liked better than regaling an appreciative audience with his accomplishments. Her, in particular.

"Naturally," he said.

"What did it entail?"

"A hunt for one of the railroad's so-called burglarproof safes and the shipment of gold it contained."

"The safe was also stolen?"

"It was, from an express office in Tuttletown."

"You recovered the gold, of course."

"Every ounce." He was so busy puffing out billows of smoke that he seemed not to notice Sabina turning in her chair to open the window behind her. "And arranged the arrest of the thieves, a pair of brothers named Schneider who owned the local icehouse."

"Ah. Was that where the gold was hidden?"

"And where I found it, yes."

"Did you have any trouble with the Schneiders?"

"A bit with one of them, not worth mentioning."

From his offhand tone and the quick fluff of his beard, Sabina had the impression that the trouble had been greater than he was letting on. It was not like him to gloss over any details of his triumphs, even those that involved personal peril. To spare her concern, perhaps—a measure of the depth of his feelings for her?

He said with a smug little smile, "You'll never guess how the Schneiders managed to open the safe."

Well, that wasn't quite true. That the brothers owned an icehouse and had hidden the loot inside it gave her a clue, but she refrained from puncturing John's conceit by offering an educated guess. She asked, "How?" and expressed proper admiration when he explained the clever method in considerable detail. When he was finished, she stroked his ego by saying, "Your usual excellent work, John."

"Cromarty and the others thought so, too. Worthy of a bonus, in my estimation, though one probably won't be forthcoming. Railroad accountants are notoriously tightfisted."

"A satisfactory fee for your time and effort, nonetheless."

"True." He polluted the room's atmosphere with more streams of noxious gray-white smoke. "And what have you been up to while I was gone?" he asked then. "Any new cases?"

"One."

"Lucrative?"

Naturally that would be his first question. "Lucrative enough. The client is a well-to-do securities broker, Winthrop Buckley."

"A case involving financial shenanigans?"

"No. His problem is personal, concerning his wife."

"The eternal triangle, eh?"

"Nothing like that." Sabina paused. "John, if you're free tomorrow night, I'd like you to attend a séance with me."

". . . Did you say séance?"

"At the Unified College of the Attuned Impulses."

His thick eyebrows lifted even higher. "Are you serious?"

"Never more."

"What the devil is the Unified College of the Attuned Impulses?"

"The guise for a spiritualism racket operated by a transplanted New Yorker named Vargas. Professor A. for Abraham Vargas, medium, spirit counselor, and womanizer."

"Womanizer?"

"By reputation and confirmed by observation and experience."

John scowled. "You mean he made advances to you?"

"Not overtly. He's too clever for that."

"How then?"

Sabina summarized her three experiences in the Turk Street house, word of the hand-holding and finger-stroking and Vargas's subtly sly innuendoes causing John's scowl to become fiercer. She also related what she had learned about the charlatan's past in New York.

"Damn the man," John said witheringly. "Communication with the dead and the rest of his stage-managed claptrap is nothing but a pile of horse . . . ah . . . horsefeathers."

"In Vargas's case, yes, I'm sure it is. But quite a lot of people believe in the existence of a spirit afterlife."

"Don't tell me you give a whit of credence to such folly?"

"I have an open mind."

"So do I, on most matters."

"But not the paranormal."

"Not a bit of it."

"Well, your skepticism is more than justified in this case,"

Sabina said. "Mr. Buckley's wife is an avid believer, however, bent on an audience with her long-departed daughter, and Vargas has convinced her that he will be able to arrange it through his self-styled Egyptian spirit guide, Angkar."

"At this séance tomorrow night?"

"Quite likely, in view of the fact that Mrs. Buckley has promised a substantial donation to his 'college' if he succeeds to her satisfaction. Five thousand dollars, to be exact."

John whistled softly. "And Buckley wants to forestall the financial loss by exposing Vargas for a fraud."

"That, and to convince his wife of the futility of her quest. Mrs. Buckley must be shown the truth in person before she'll accept it."

"And you propose to accomplish this by exposing his spirit-world manifestations for the tricks they are."

"Just so. It shouldn't be too difficult, thanks to Madame Louella's tutoring—I spent half an hour with her earlier today. I expect I could manage it alone, but the two of us working in concert would ensure success."

"Your safety and that of the Buckleys, as well. There is no telling what scoundrels like this Vargas are capable of when unmasked, even in front of witnesses."

"You'll come with me, then? I paved the way this morning by asking Vargas if he minded my bringing my cousin with me. Of course he had no objection to another twenty-five-dollar donation."

"Unless Mr. Boggs has urgent need of me, yes, I will. Attending a séance will be a new experience for both of us." John's glower modulated into one of his basilisk smiles. "The prospect of putting a philandering flimflammer who preys on vulnerable women out of commission warms my cockles."

Sabina gazed fondly at him. His ready agreement was gratifying; she had expected him to balk some at the suggestion, to have to cajole him into accepting. Another measure of his feelings toward her and their budding intimacy? It pleased her to believe so.

11

QUINCANNON

A streetcar deposited him at Fifth and Mission, in front of the San Francisco Mint, shortly past nine on Saturday morning. The two-story Greek Revival and Doric-style structure, known as the Granite Lady even though only its base and basement were constructed of granite—the external and upper stories were of sandstone—had been erected in 1874, a much larger replacement of the original mint built during the '49 Gold Rush. In its granite bowels, millions upon millions of dollars of gold bullion was refined and made into ingots and into coins as needed. It was also where the second-floor offices of the Secret Service, presided over by Mr. Boggs, were located.

As always when he had occasion to come here, Quincannon had mixed feelings as he climbed the broad front steps to the entrance. His memories of his time as a senior Service operative were both good and bad. Until the incident in Arizona nearly eight years ago, in which a stray bullet from his sidearm during a pitched gun battle with a gang of counterfeiters had struck and killed a pregnant bystander, he had gloried in his government work and expected to remain with the Service until retirement age.

But the weight of guilt over the deaths of the innocent woman and her unborn child had plunged him into a downward spiral of alcohol consumption that eventually would have destroyed his career, had it not been for the unwavering support of Mr. Boggs. And meeting Sabina during the course of separate but convergent investigations that had taken them both to the mountain settlement of Silver Springs, Idaho. His decision to leave the Service and open his own private agency, and Sabina's acceptance of his offer to join forces with him, had firmed his resolve to put a permanent end to his drinking. And though Boggs had been sorry to lose him, the decision had nonetheless met with the chief's wholehearted approval. The guilt remained, but Quincannon had succeeded in walling it off in a corner of his mind so that, except for an occasional nightmare, it no longer plagued him.

The mint had a central pedimented portico flanked by projecting wings and a completely enclosed courtyard that contained a working well. The entrance to the basement where the gold was stored and refined was well guarded, but the main floor and the one above were open to the public. Quincannon circled halfway around the courtyard, climbed the staircase to the second floor, and found his way to the Secret Service suite. That door was kept locked at all times; he rapped on it, announced himself, and was admitted immediately.

Mr. Boggs waited in his large, cluttered sanctum. It had been nearly a year since Quincannon had last seen his former chief, a chance meeting at the Ferry Building; Boggs hadn't changed an iota since then, and except for being a little grayer, a little heavier, hardly at all since their working days together. His bulbous nose glowed like a red bung in a keg of whiskey, and as usual one of his favored long-nine cigars jutted from a corner of his mouth.

His handclasp, as always, was as iron-hard as his will. "Good to see you again, John," he said, "even in pressing circumstances."

"And you as well, sir."

"I'm sorry I wasn't here when you came yesterday. Called away on a matter not related to the one I wired you about. You remember the Darrow case, of course."

Quincannon nodded. "I'm not likely ever to forget Long Nick Darrow, even after ten years."

"I reread your report of the incident on the Seattle waterfront. No doubt in your mind then that Darrow died from his wound, submersion in the icy harbor, or a combination of both."

"None, despite the fact that the body was never found. There hasn't been a whisper of him since, so far as I know."

"No. But he may have survived, unlikely as it seems."

"What makes you think he might have?"

"I'll let you judge for yourself, John."

From a drawer in his cigar-burned desk Boggs took a banknote and a thick-lensed magnifying glass, both of which he handed to Quincannon. The note was a hundred-dollar series 1891 silver certificate bearing the portrait of James Monroe. Quincannon examined both sides of it through the glass.

"Counterfeit," he said. "Nearly perfect."

"Recognize the coney work?"

"It appears to be familiar, yes."

"Take a closer look."

Quincannon did so. The counterfeit had been made, he judged, using one of the new processes of photolithography or photoengraving. The latter, most likely; the quality of reproduction was excellent, though not remarkably so, and the note bore the rich dark lines of genuine government bills. There was a certain loss of detail, too, of the sort caused by the erratic biting of acid during the etching process. The loss of detail was one thing that marked the hundred as bogus. There were others, too: the Treasury seal was lightly inked and looked pink instead of carmine; the bill's dimensions were a fraction of an inch too small in both width and length; and the formation of the letters spelling "James" under President Monroe's portrait showed evidence of either poor etchwork or acid burn. All of these flaws were minor enough to escape the naked eye, even a well-trained one. A glass such as this one was necessary to spot them.

The paper appeared to be genuine, carrying both the "U.S." watermark in several places and the large, prominent-colored silk threads used by the government's official papermaker, Crane & Co. of Dalton, Massachusetts. This would have been startling, given the rigid Treasury Department safeguards against the theft of banknote paper, except for two things. One was that the bogus bill was a mite too thick. The other was that crisscrossing the engraved scroll lines were fine, colorless marks that ran in seeming confusion—the imprints of previous engraving.

When Quincannon lowered the glass, Boggs said, "Well?"

"Certainly looks like Darrow's work. But it's not old enough to have been a leftover from the Seattle operation just come to light."

"No, it's not. But would you say it's the same expert job of bleaching and bill-splitting?"

"Perhaps. Close, though the paste appears to have been applied a bit too thickly."

"You haven't lost your eye. I compared it to one of Darrow's bogus certificates from our archives. Except for the paste, I found the two to be quite similar, as well."

"How many of these have been confiscated?"

"Sixteen, so far."

"All here in the city?"

"No. Eleven here, five in the East Bay."

"The first one when?"

"Just last week. The president of the First Western Bank spotted it and brought it to us."

"No other counterfeit hundreds like this one turned up in the past decade, I take it?"

"None that have come to our attention. And they surely would have during that time, sooner or later."

Quincannon studied the bill again through the glass. "The plates that made this were certainly photoengraved."

"I agree. Every letter and line cut into the metal by hand, following the tracings of the photographic image—the same process used in the Bureau of Printing and Engraving. Except that Darrow, if it was Darrow, didn't have the advantage of a geometric lathe."

"But the process hadn't been perfected yet when he was operating in the Pacific Northwest. The forgery method in those days was to place a genuine hundred on a zinc plate and transfer its ink to the metal with a solvent, then engrave the plate by following the inked lines and letters."

"Anastatic printing," Boggs said, nodding. "A long, slow, and imperfect process. Besides, according to your report those anastatic plates of his were destroyed in the fire along with the rest of his equipment."

"They must have been, yes."

"So in order to begin afresh, he would have had to have had new ones made, and photoengraving being faster and more certain, naturally he would have found an engraver able to employ that method."

"You've had your operatives canvassing printing and engraving shops in the city and outlying areas, of course."

"And with no luck so far. There are a damned lot of them, and as usual we're shorthanded. Still more than two dozen to be checked, better than half of those outside the city." Boggs shook his head. "A futile endeavor, I'm afraid, without some indication of guilt that would permit us to conduct a thorough search of the premises."

"The shop would have to have a fairly large printing press to produce bills of this caliber," Quincannon mused. "That should narrow the field a bit. Unless . . ."

"Unless the operation here is similar to the one in Seattle, set up in a warehouse or abandoned building rather than a regular printing shop. Darrow's a sly fox. He could have bought the press secondhand somewhere close by, or had it shipped in in parts and reassembled."

"Any koniaker could've thought of that. What about the man passing the queer? Or have there been more than one?"

"At least two."

"No useful descriptions?"

"One, provided by the owner of an Oakland haberdashery. A middle-aged, heavyset fellow with two distinguishing features: a thick black mustache and eyes of a different color—one brown, one blue."

"A traceable trait, that last, if he has a criminal record."

"He doesn't, so far as we've been able to determine," Boggs said. "The few known felons with different-color eyes either don't match the rest of this one's description, or are dead or locked away in prison. Our one hope is that he continues to shove queer and another sharp-eyed banker or businessman recognizes him and he's caught before he can get away. Flyers have been distributed to every bank and large business establishment on both sides of the Bay and as far south as San Jose. But for all we know, Darrow or whoever is running the game is using several passers rather than just a handful. That was how he operated in the Northwest."

Quincannon said, "I still find it difficult to believe that Darrow is alive and back in business after a ten-year hiatus. The man responsible could be someone who learned bleaching and bill-splitting from him."

"I've considered that," Boggs said. "But it couldn't be any of his henchmen in Seattle. Two were killed in the raid and warehouse fire, including his engraver, Cooley, and of the remaining two, one died in prison and the other is still incarcerated. The fact remains, John, that the coney work could still be Darrow's, with the slight differences in bill-splitting technique explained by ten years' advancement in age."

"You've checked with the authorities in Seattle regarding Darrow, of course."

"The authorities in Tacoma, Portland, and other Pacific Northwest cities, as well. Wired the description of him you included in your report and all the known details of his past activities and known associates. None of the agencies has a record of anyone who might be Darrow or of counterfeiting or other crimes during the past decade that he might have been involved in. Frustrating, but hardly conclusive."

"I don't suppose the local constabulary could shed any light on the situation."

Boggs said, "Hah. Those inept dolts couldn't catch wind of a clever crook if he went around town advertising his crimes on a signboard. You know that as well as I do."

"All too well." Quincannon handed the counterfeit hundred back to his former chief, raked fingers through his beard. "So why have you called on me, Mr. Boggs? It can't be just because of my familiarity with Darrow and his methods."

"That, and three other reasons." Boggs licked his dead cigar back to the other side of his mouth, pushed his bulk upright from the corner of the desk where he had parked it. "First, you were the agent responsible for shutting down his operation and severely if not lethally wounding him. If he is still alive, he may harbor a desire for revenge. Which could be the reason he chose to set up a new coney game in this area."

"After so much time has passed? That seems highly doubtful."

"But not impossible. It would depend on where he's been and what he has been up to since '87."

"Granted. And the other two reasons?"

"Second, Darrow was a shadowy figure in those days, one who avoided intimate contact with anyone outside his gang. The Seattle operatives who accompanied you on the raid had only glimpses of him, and none of those still alive recall him clearly. You're the only man we know who had close personal contact with him."

Quincannon's memory disgorged a half-forgotten image of the counterfeiter. Long Nick Darrow had been some forty years of age in 1887, lean and muscular in a predatory way, his shaggy hair, beetled brows, and horseshoe-shaped beard (sans mustache) a dark auburn color. And his brown eyes were as cold and unblinking as a viper's.

"Seen only twice under stressful circumstances," he pointed out. "A man's appearance can change in a number of ways, for a number of reasons, in ten years. Darrow could pass me on the street and I might not have a glimmer of recognition."

"On the other hand, you might have more than a glimmer if you were to stand face-to-face with him. You're our only reliable witness nonetheless."

"And reason number three?"

Boggs relit his dead cigar with a flint desk lighter, made a distasteful face, and screwed the butt into a glass ashtray. He spat out a shred of soggy tobacco before saying, "I hate to admit this, but you have certain sources of information not available to representatives of the United States government."

Quincannon's mouth quirked sardonically. "Meaning five years of having by necessity consorted with all manner of underworld types in and out of the city."

"Putting it baldly, yes. You have the contacts and confidence of individuals who might know something that would assist us in getting to the bottom of this new coney racket, whether Darrow is behind it or not."

"For a price, if so. I don't suppose the Service would underwrite my expenses?"

Boggs gave him a stony "don't ask foolish questions" look. At length he said, "Well, John? Can I count on your cooperation?"

"You knew you could, sir, or you wouldn't have taken me into your confidence. I despise counterfeiters as much as I did when I was with the Service, and if Long Nick Darrow is still alive, I want to know it as much as you do. I'll do everything in my power to help find out."

12

QUINCANNON

The Redemption, Ezra Bluefield's saloon and restaurant on Ellis Street in the Uptown Tenderloin, was nothing at all like the rowdy Barbary Coast deadfall called the Scarlet Lady that he had previously owned, either in appearance or in the clientele to which it catered. It had been and still was a reasonably respectable establishment among the hodgepodge of hurdy-gurdy dance halls, variety-show theaters, gambling parlors, and sporting houses that infested the area and made it, in the eyes of many, a somewhat less dangerous version of the Coast.

An ex-miner in the rough-and-tumble goldfields of the Mother Lode, Bluefield had bought the Scarlet Lady from the widow of its former owner, who had been stabbed to death in a dispute over a prostitute. It had been a notorious crimping joint in those days, one of the many saloons in which seamen were served drinks laced with laudanum or chloral hydrate and then carted off to be sold to unscrupulous ship captains in need of crews. The

Sailor's Union of the Pacific had put an end to that, forcing the temporary closure of the Scarlet Lady. When enough bribes had been paid and Bluefield reopened the place, it was as a simple deadfall where customers were relieved of their cash by "pretty waiter girls," bunco ploys, and rigged games of chance. Knockout drops were used only on rare occasions.

Unlike other deadfall owners, Bluefield remained aloof from all this. He employed several bouncers and vanished into his private office whenever trouble broke out, which was more or less nightly. It wasn't that he was a coward; he'd had his share of fistfights and cutting scrapes in his gold-mining days. He had no qualms about reaping the Scarlet Lady's profits, but not for the usual profligate reasons; he saved his money in order to fulfill a long-standing desire to own a better class of watering hole in a more reputable neighborhood. He had had his fill of catering to the dregs of society, wishing instead to cultivate the company and goodwill of more or less honest citizens.

Quincannon had once prevented a rival saloon owner from shooting Bluefield during a territorial quarrel, and had again helped him by writing a letter of reference to the former owners of the Redemption; in exchange, Bluefield had supplied information gleaned from his numerous contacts in the Barbary Coast and elsewhere. Even now that he was firmly established in his new place of business, he still had his finger on the pulse of the city's underworld and could be counted on, as long as the frequency was limited, to grant Quincannon's requests for favors.

It was a few minutes shy of noon when Quincannon arrived at the Redemption. Bluefield's establishment was his third stop since leaving the mint. The first two had been brief contacts with two of the more trustworthy individuals who supplied him with bits and pieces of information about criminals and criminal activities in the city: Slewfoot, the "blind" news vendor, and Galway, the crafty desk clerk in a cheap hotel on the fringe of the Coast. Neither knew of anyone who answered the description of Long Nick Darrow or who possessed a pair of mismatched eyes.

Many of the Tenderloin's buildings bore fancy signs and gaudy advertisements, and a few such as Charles Riley's House of Chance were lit up at night by energized gas in large electric discharge lamps, but the Redemption's façade was unadorned except for a small, tasteful sign in its plate-glass front window. The interior was likewise tastefully appointed, with none of the frills and furbelows such as nude or near-nude paintings that decorated other establishments in the neighborhood. The saloon section was free of gambling layouts, percentage girls, and rowdy behavior. Strictly a place for those interested in medium-quality dining, drinks that were neither doctored nor watered down, and a convivial atmosphere. Bluefield had kept his promise of semirespectability, and was so proud of the "gentleman" publican and restaurateur he had become that he no longer hid away in his office, but circulated constantly among his patrons, glad-handing regulars and newcomers alike.

Bluefield could usually be found in the Redemption from its late-morning opening until its late-night closing; today was no exception. He was in the restaurant section, just sitting down to his favorite noonday meal of a plate of oysters on the half shell and a foaming mug of lager. A big man, Bluefield, with an enormous handlebar mustache the ends of which were waxed to sword points, and a chest as broad as a stallion's. His taste in suits and cravats had improved considerably since his Scarlet Lady days, though he still favored mustard-colored waistcoats.

He waved Quincannon to a chair, saying, "Hello, lad. And how be you this fine day?"

"Well and good. And you?"

"Likewise. In the pink. Care to have a meal with me? Fresh from the Bay, these oysters, and as succulent as they come."

Quincannon couldn't very well refuse. Besides, he was hungry. He took the proffered chair, and when Bluefield summoned a waiter, ordered a dozen oysters on the half shell and a glass of warm clam juice.

"Clam juice." Bluefield's nose wrinkled. "I don't see how you can drink that stuff."

"An acquired taste."

"Not one I'll ever acquire." Then, cannily, "Well, lad, what brings you to the Redemption? Come to pay a social call on old Ezra, or is it to beg yet another favor?"

"The former," Quincannon said, stretching the truth, "and the answers to a few questions. I know I've used up my quota of favors—"

Bluefield waved a dismissive hand; he was in a jovial mood. "You have, but I don't mind having my brain picked. But not until after we've put on the feedbag."

He waited for Quincannon to be served, hungrily eyeing his oysters and his beer. The second plate of oysters and clam juice arrived in swift fashion; Bluefield's employees didn't tarry, lest they be subjected to the old reprobate's wrathful tongue. As soon as Quincannon's meal was set down, Bluefield picked up a shell, inhaled oyster and juice, and then washed them down with a large draught of beer.

Quincannon found the oysters to be every bit as good as advertised. The clam juice, however, left much to be desired—no place seasoned it nearly as well as Hoolihan's Saloon, his favorite watering hole—but he praised it nonetheless. Bluefield beamed at him in return.

When all the shells on both plates were empty, Bluefield drained the last of his beer and sat back contentedly. In his Scarlet Lady days he would likely have emitted a loud belch; now he merely patted his lips and removed foam from his mustache with a linen napkin.

"Now then," he said. "These questions of yours. To do with what this time?"

"A coney game. The shoving of counterfeit hundred-dollar notes."

"Coney game, eh? Don't tell me you're working for the government again?"

"Not exactly," Quincannon hedged. "Have you heard of such a game in progress locally, Ezra?"

"Can't say that I have, no."

"Does the name Long Nick Darrow ring any bells?"

"Darrow, Darrow." Bluefield wagged his head. "Nary a tinkle. Is he the one running the game?"

"That remains to be determined." Quincannon described Darrow as he'd looked ten years ago, finishing with, "He'd be close to fifty now."

"You want me to put out feelers, eh?"

"If you would, but as discreetly as possible."

"Easy enough done," Bluefield said. "Anything else?"

"One of the bill-passers had one brown eye and one blue eye—a thickset man, middle-aged, sporting a thick black mustache. Would you know of anyone who answers that description?"

"One brown eye, one blue eye. Well, now." Bluefield nibbled at his long lower lip while he searched his memory. At length he snapped his fingers and said, "Paddy Lasher."

The name meant nothing to Quincannon. "Who would he be?"

"A rascal I knew once upon a time."

"What manner of rascal?"

"Shanghai crimp. Only man I ever saw with different-colored eyes. No lip whiskers when I knew him, but that was a long time ago."

Quincannon didn't need to ask how Bluefield had known Lasher; he wouldn't have got a straight answer if he had asked. Bluefield was ashamed of having been part and parcel of the crimping racket for even a short time and refused to discuss it.

"Have you any idea what Lasher has been up to since his shanghaiing days?"

"None, lad. Years since I've seen his ugly puss. He might have left the city, or been terminated by a bullet or a blade. If he's still here and above the sod, he's stayed in the shadows."

"Do you know if he had a criminal record of any kind?"

"In those days, he didn't. Proud of the fact that he'd stayed free of the law's clutches."

If Paddy Lasher still had no criminal record, he was not one of the trio of brown-eye/blue-eye felons that Boggs had investigated and dismissed. The gap was wide between shanghaiing and counterfeiting, but when a mug was denied his primary source of illegal income, he gravitated to any other sort of illegal enterprise that presented itself. It was entirely possible that Lasher was now engaged in shoving queer.

"Did he have any pals when you knew him?"

"Hah! Nobody short of a half-wit would have palled with the likes of him," Bluefield said. "Want me to put out the word about him, too, eh?"

"I'd appreciate it, Ezra."

"Done." Then, as Quincannon pushed back his chair, "You owe me a favor now, lad, and whatever it might be I intend to collect before you ask another. You won't forget that, will you?"

"I won't forget."

In front of the bathroom mirror in his Leavenworth Street flat that evening, Quincannon finished tying a satisfactory knot in his black silk cravat and then buttoned the waistcoat of his conservative three-piece suit. He preferred decorative vests, which he felt gave him a more dashing, somewhat roguish appearance, but Sabina had reminded him of the ruse of a family in mourning that she had concocted for her sessions with Professor A.-for-Abraham Vargas. It wouldn't do for a member of the fictitious Milford clan to attend the séance wearing the likes of a dark blue silk vest decorated with orange nasturtiums, his personal favorite.

He donned the suit jacket and again regarded himself in the glass. Even in sedate clothing, he decided he cut a rather handsome figure. Not that that would matter once they arrived at the Unified College of the Attuned Impulses (silly damned name!) and he embarked on his role as a Milford cousin, but it was important that Sabina should be pleased with both his appearance and his company.

Ah, Sabina. The depth of his feelings for her was stimulating but also a little disconcerting. Here he was, a lifelong bachelor who had indulged in a string of free-and-easy liaisons with a variety of comely young ladies, and whose future had promised more of the same well into his dotage, and he had eyes for no one other than his partner. Every other woman, no matter how attractive or available, seemed to pale to insignificance when compared to Sabina. Seduction had been his primary interest in the beginning; now his passion for her had evolved into something much more tender and abiding.

Something . . . permanent? Such as marriage?

The word "marriage," writ large in his mind, produced a small shudder. John Frederick Quincannon, married. Such a possibility would have been utterly inconceivable five, even four years ago, despite the closeness of his professional relationship with Sabina. He had always viewed himself as an indestructible lone wolf, never to be tied down, forever free until he realized his dream of dying in bed at the age of ninety while consummating one last conquest. He told himself that he was incapable of fidelity, that marriage would damage if not doom Carpenter and Quincannon, Professional Detective Services. No matter how much two people cared for each other, they couldn't live as well as work together.

But the arguments were not nearly as potent as they had once been. His resolve was weakening. The more time he spent with Sabina away from the office, the more he wanted to be with her.

What to do about this confusing conundrum?

He didn't know, couldn't make up his mind.

"John Frederick," he said to his mirror image, "you're a blasted coward when it comes to affairs of the heart."

The image nodded its hirsute head in agreement.

13

SABINA

The séance was scheduled to begin at eight o'clock. By arrangement that afternoon, John came in a cab to fetch her shortly past seven. As on her previous visits to the lair of the Unified College of the Attuned Impulses, she had dressed in a dark-colored outfit overlain with a heavy gray cape in deference to the night's chill. A thin, wind-driven mist writhed among the tops of trees and the upper sections of Russian Hill, gave street lamps an ethereal, wrapped-in-gossamer effect. An appropriate backdrop, Sabina thought wryly, for the summoning of spirits from beyond the veil.

John was in an introspective mood tonight, curiously so since he had been talkative enough earlier in reporting the details of his conversation with Mr. Boggs. Yet he was also more than usually attentive. He sat close to her in the lamplit cab as they rode down Van Ness Avenue, an intimacy she not only allowed but enjoyed. After a few failed attempts to draw him out, she remained companionably silent herself. There was no need for any further discussion of their plans for the evening ahead; all the necessary details were already in place.

A snarl of traffic impeded the hansom's progress so that it was nearly eight o'clock when they arrived at 3601 Turk Street. Two expensive carriages, a large landau and a smaller, high-wheeled phaeton, were parked in front of the small house; evidently the Buckleys and the Cobbs were already in attendance. The mist was thicker here. Foghorns moaning on the Bay had a lonely, lost-soul sound. When John helped her alight from the cab, the bitter-sharp wind nipped at her cheeks and nearly tore her hat free of its pinnings before she could clamp it down with one gloved hand.

They paused briefly at the gate while he peered at the sign affixed to its post. "Bah," he muttered under his breath. "How can any sane person believe in such hokum?"

"Self-deception is the most powerful kind."

He made a derisive noise in his throat, a sound Sabina had once likened to the rumbling snarl of a mastiff.

She said, "If you enter scowling and muttering, you'll give the game away. We're here as devotees, not skeptics."

"Devotees of claptrap."

"John, need I remind you that Winthrop Buckley is paying us handsomely for this evening's work?"

His expression smoothed. "Not to worry, my dear. I'll play my role properly until the time comes for masks off."

He took her arm as they passed through the gate, mounted the stairs to the lantern-lit porch, and twisted the doorbell. Annabelle appeared almost immediately. She wore the black cowled robe to-night, her braided and coiled hair piled high atop her head, her lips painted crimson; the sharp contrast of the bloody mouth color with her pale skin was surely intended to enhance her otherworldly connection, but to Sabina's eye it succeeded only in making her resemble an animated corpse.

"Good evening, Annabelle."

"You have arrived just in time," the woman said in her sepulchral voice. "The séance will soon begin."

"An unavoidable delay. This is my cousin, John Milford."

"How do you do," John said with a small, polite smile. Playing his role now as promised, not that Sabina had expected otherwise.

Annabelle acknowledged him with a dip of her chin. Then she said, "Enter, friends," in a not very friendly tone.

Inside, she took Sabina's cape and John's Chesterfield and hung them on the coattree. After which she led them to the parlor, announced them, and immediately glided away through the black curtain at the far end.

Professor A. Vargas was among the others gathered there. Like Annabelle, he wore a long flowing black robe and the usual white amulet. Winthrop Buckley, dressed in a tailored suit with a velvet-lapeled coat and a high regency collar, gave no indication of recognition when his bespectacled gaze met Sabina's. He seemed a trifle ill at ease, as if he wished the evening's business were already finished. His wife, Margaret, was gray-haired, portly, tightly corseted into a dark blue gown; her attention was entirely focused on Vargas, her gaze as rapt as that of a supplicant in the presence of a saint. The Cobbs, Oliver and Grace, were also well dressed and wore expressions of eager anticipation. The doctor bore a rather startling resemblance to the "literary hangman," Ambrose Bierce; his blond-haired wife was much younger and decorous in an overly buxom and overly rouged fashion. Despite her demeanor, Sabina had the sense that she was more predatory than devout.

Vargas greeted Sabina with smiling courtesy, pressing his lips to the back of her hand—a familiarity that caused John's eyes to narrow. Declaration of his false identity triggered a round of introductions, after which the bogus medium fixed him with his piercing gaze.

"I trust that you, too, are a sincere believer in the world beyond the veil, sir?" he said.

"Yes, though I have never attended a séance before. I understand they are quite enlightening."

"Indeed they are. There are many anxious friends in the spirit world who desire to communicate with the living."

"Are the spirits friendly tonight?" Mrs. Buckley asked.

"The Auras are uncertain. Angkar perceives antagonistic vibrations among the benign."

"Oh, Professor!"

"Do not fear," Vargas said. "Even if a malevolent spirit should cross the border, no harm will come to you or any of us. Angkar will protect us."

"But will my Bernice's spirit be allowed through if there is a malevolent force present?"

"Or my brother Gregory's," Sabina said.

"Yes," Dr. Cobb said, "and my cherished mother's."

Vargas patted Sabina's arm reassuringly. "Your impulses have been properly attuned, Mrs. Milford. As have yours, Mrs. Buckley and yours, Dr. Cobb. It is my great hope that each of your departed loved ones will appear, though naturally I cannot be certain until the veil has been lifted and Angkar has been summoned. Have faith, dear ladies, good doctor."

John's dislike for the charlatan was well concealed, but Sabina knew him well enough to tell that he was in no way impressed by the man's pose and glib patter.

To his mind, Vargas was just another confidence trickster to be unmasked and put out of business. His voice was as blandly hopeful as his expression when he asked, "Isn't there anything you can do to prevent a malevolent spirit from crossing over?"

"Alas, no." Vargas then repeated the sentence he had spoken to Sabina at their first meeting, word for word. "I am merely a teacher of the light and truth of theocratic unity, merely an operator between the astral plane and this mortal sphere."

Grace Cobb touched the wrist that protruded from the sleeve of his robe, her fingers lingering almost caressingly. The intimate way in which his fingers caressed hers in return, and the smoldering quality of the look he bestowed upon her, made Sabina wonder if Mrs. Cobb had been one of his conquests. It wouldn't surprise her to learn that she had.

"We have faith in you, Professor," the woman said.

"In Angkar, dear lady," Vargas told her. "Place your faith in Angkar and the spirit world."

"Oh, Professor Vargas," Mrs. Buckley gushed, "you're so wise in so many ways."

Annabelle reappeared as silently as she had gone. "All is in readiness, Professor," she announced, and without waiting for a response, glided away again.

"Good friends," Vargas said, "before we enter the séance room may I accept your most kind and welcome donations to the Unified College of the Attuned Impulses so that we may succeed in our humble efforts to bring the psychic and material planes into closer harmony?"

John paid for Sabina and himself. If he had not been assured of having the greenbacks returned before the evening ended, or of reimbursement from their client if the debunking of Vargas's flimflam failed to go as planned, he would no doubt have handed them over grudgingly. Mr. Buckley was tight-lipped as he paid; the covert glance he directed at Sabina was a mute plea for the promised success. Only Dr. Cobb ponied up with what appeared to be genuine enthusiasm.

Vargas casually dropped the wad of bills onto a table, as if money mattered not in the slightest to him personally, then led the group out of the parlor, down the gloomy hallway, and into a large room next to the one in which his consultations were held. The "spirit room," as he called it, contained quite a few more furnishings and props than the other, these of greater variety and a more exotic nature.

The floor was covered by an Oriental carpet of dark blue and black design. More curtains made of the same ebon material as the two swindlers' robes blotted a pair of windows; the gaslight had been turned down even lower than it had been in the consulting room, creating shadows in corners and along the low ceiling. The overheated air was permeated with the same incense that had tormented Sabina on her previous visits. The unpleasant scent in this room came from a different, larger burner perched on the fireplace mantel—a horsey-looking bronze monstrosity with tusks as well as equine teeth and a shaggy mane and beard.

The room's centerpiece was an oval, highly polished table around which seven chairs were arranged. Six of them were straight-backed; the seventh was a twin of the high-seated one in which Vargas sat facing his acolytes during their individual consultations, except that its arms were raised on a level with that of the tabletop. In the middle of the table stood a clear-glass jar, inside of which a tiny silver bell was suspended.

Along the walls were a short, narrow cabinet of Oriental design, made of teak with an intricately inlayed top; a tall-backed rococo love seat; and an alabaster pedestal atop which sat a hideous bronze statue of an Egyptian male in full headdress—a representation, evidently, of the mythical Angkar. Atop the cabinet were a silver tray containing several bottles of various sizes and shapes, a tambourine, and a stack of children's school slates with black wooden frames. Propped against the wall nearby was an ordinary-looking three-stringed guitar. And on the high seat of the armchair lay a coil of sturdy rope Sabina estimated to be some three yards in length.

When everyone was inside and loosely grouped near the table, Vargas closed the door, produced a large brass key from a pocket in his robe, and proceeded with a flourish to turn the key in the latch. After which he brought the key to the cabinet and set it beside the tray in plain sight. While this was being done, Sabina saw John, at the rear of the assemblage, ease back to the door and test it with a hand behind his back to determine if it was in fact

121

locked. It was, for he caught her eye and dipped his chin affir-
matively.

Still at the sideboard, Vargas announced that before the séance commenced two final preparations were necessary. Would
one of the "friends of Angkar" be so kind as to assist him in the
first of these? John stepped forward just ahead of Dr. Cobb.

The bogus medium said, "Mr. Milford, will you kindly examine each of the slates you see before you and tell us if they are as
they seem—ordinary writing slates?"

John examined them more carefully than any of the devotees
would have. "Quite ordinary," he said.

"Select two, if you please, then write your name on each with
this slate pencil. Once that has been done, place them together
and tie them securely with your handkerchief."

When John had complied, Vargas claimed the bound slates
and put them in the middle of the stack. "If the spirits are willing," he said, "a message will be left for you beneath the signatures. Perhaps from your cousin Gregory or another loved one
who has passed beyond the veil, perhaps from a friendly spirit
who may be in sympathy with your psychic impulses even though
I have not had the opportunity to properly attune them. Discarnate forces are never predictable, you understand."

John nodded solemnly, as though this gibberish made perfect
sense to him.

"We may now be seated and form the mystic circle."

When everyone had selected and was standing behind a chair,
Sabina to Vargas's immediate left and John directly across from
him, both by prearrangement, Vargas again called for a volun-

teer. This time it was Dr. Cobb who stepped forward first. Vargas handed him the coiled rope and seated himself in the high chair, his forearms flat on the chair arms with only his wrists and hands extended beyond the edges. He then instructed Cobb to bind him securely to the chair—arms, legs, and chest—using as many knots as possible. Sabina and John both watched closely as this was done. Once again their gazes met briefly and both dipped their chins to acknowledge that they had spotted the gaffe in this phase of the professor's game.

Dr. Cobb, with Buckley's help, moved Vargas's chair closer to the table, so that his hands and wrists rested on the surface. Smiling, the fake medium asked them all to take their seats. As Sabina sat down she bumped against the table, then reached down to feel one of its legs. As she'd expected, the table was much less heavy than it appeared to be at a glance. She stretched out a leg and with the toe of her shoe explored the carpet. The floor beneath seemed to be solid, but the nap was thick enough so that she couldn't be certain.

Vargas instructed everyone to spread their hands, the fingers of the right to grasp the left wrist of the person next to them, thus creating a complete circle. His warm, dry hand closed over Sabina's wrist; she in turn clutched the moist wrist of Margaret Buckley seated on her right.

"Once we commence," Vargas said then, "attempt to empty your minds of all thought, to keep them as blank as the surfaces of the slates throughout. And remember, good friends, you must not move either hands or feet during the séance—you must not under any circumstances break the mystic circle. To do so could have grave consequences. There have been instances where in-attention and disobedience have proven fatal to sensitives while in a deep trance."

He closed his eyes, let his chin lower slowly to his chest. And the performance began.

14

SABINA

Nearly a minute passed in silence while Vargas pretended to place himself in a mesmeric trance. Then he commenced a whispering chant in English punctuated by what Sabina took to be simulated Egyptian, in which he called for the door to the spirit world to open and the shades of the departed to pass through and reveal their presence. While this was going on, the lights began to dim as if in response to his exhortations. The phenomenon elicited a shivery gasp from Margaret Buckley, but there was nothing otherworldly about it. Gaslight in one room was easily controlled from another—in this case by Annabelle at a prearranged time or on some sort of signal.

The shadows congealed until the room was in utter darkness. Vargas's chanting ceased abruptly; the silence deepened as it lengthened. Long minutes passed with no sounds except for the somewhat asthmatic breathing of Winthrop Buckley, the rustle of a dress or shuffle of a foot on the carpet. A palpable suspense began to build. Sabina could feel tiny beads of perspiration on her upper lip, not from any tension but from the overheated air. She was not given to fancies, but she had to admit that there was an eerie quality to sitting in total blackness this way, waiting for something to happen. Spiritualist mediums counted on this reaction, of course. The more keyed up their dupes became, the more eager they were to believe in the incredible things they were about to witness; and the more eager they were, the more easily they could be fooled by their own senses.

Someone coughed, a sudden sharp sound that made even Sabina twitch involuntarily. She thought the cough had come from Vargas, but in such stifling darkness you couldn't be certain of the direction of any sound. Even when he spoke again, the words might have come from anywhere in the room.

"Angkar is with us." His normally stentorian voice was muted now, almost a monotone. "I feel his presence."

Mrs. Buckley stirred and her knee bumped against Sabina's. The contact brought forth another of the woman's shivery gasps.

"Will you speak to us tonight, Angkar? Will you answer our questions in the language of the dead and guide us among your fellow spirits? Please grant our request. All here with me are friends."

The silver bell inside the jar rang once, soft and clear.

"Angkar has consented. He will speak, he will lead us. He will ring the bell once for 'yes' to each question he is asked, twice for 'no,' for that is the language of the dead. Will someone ask him a question?"

"I will," Dr. Cobb's voice answered. "Angkar, is my dear

mother Elena Richmond Cobb well and happy on the Other Side?"

The bell tinkled once.

"Will she appear to us in her spirit form?"

Yes.

"Will she do so tonight?"

Silence.

Vargas said in his droning monotone, "Angkar is unable to answer that question yet. He asks for another."

Mrs. Buckley obliged immediately. Yes, her beloved Bernice was still well and happy among the spirits. Yes, she was present. Yes, she would make every effort to communicate.

Sabina spoke up next, asking in anxious tones, "Angkar, tell me please, is my brother Gregory with you? Gregory Milford."

Yes, he is one of us.

"Is he among you tonight?"

No.

"Why won't he come and speak to me?"

Silence.

Vargas said, "Yes, Angkar, I understand. The spirit of Gregory Milford has yet to fully adapt to life on the astral plane."

"But I must speak to him." Sabina made her voice sharp, agitated. "I must!"

John chimed in with, "Yes, it's vital, absolutely vital that we consult with Gregory tonight."

Without warning, the table seemed to stir and tremble. Its smooth surface rippled; a faint creak sounded from somewhere underneath. In the next instant the table tilted sideways, causing the bell to tinkle furiously; turned and rocked and wobbled as if it had been injected with a life of its own. Margaret Buckley emitted another of her gasps, her moist fingers clutching Sabina's wrist tightly. Grace Cobb murmured something in a startled undertone.

The agitated movements continued for several seconds, then stopped abruptly. The table lifted completely off the floor, seemed to float in the air for another two or three heartbeats before finally thudding back onto the carpet.

"Angkar has been angered by the Milfords' inappropriate demands. He may now deny us further communication and return to his exalted place in the Afterworld."

Mrs. Buckley cried, "Oh, no, please, he mustn't go!"

"Silence! We must do nothing more to disturb him or the discarnate plane or the consequences may be dire. Do not move or speak. Do not break the circle."

The stuffy blackness closed down again. The silence was acute, as if breaths were being held around the table; even Mr. Buckley's soft wheezing had ceased. It was an effort for Sabina to remain still.

A sound burst forth, a jingling that was not of the silver bell inside the jar. The tambourine that had been on the sideboard, closer now, almost as if it were wavering in the air nearby. Its metal jingles sounded in an eerily discordant way.

"Angkar is still present." Vargas's droning whisper was fervent. "He has forgiven Mrs. Milford her outburst, permitted us one more chance to communicate with the spirits he has brought with him."

Mrs. Buckley: "Praise Angkar! Praise the spirits!"

The shaking and jingling of the tambourine ended. All at once a ghostly light appeared at a distance overhead, pale and vaporous; remained stationary for a few seconds, then commenced a swirling motion that created faint luminous streaks on the wall of black. Mrs. Buckley made an ecstatic throat noise. The swirls slowed, the light still again for a moment; then it began to rise until it seemed to hover just below the ceiling; and at last it faded away entirely. Other lights, mere pinpricks, flicked on and off, moving this way and that as if a handful of fireflies had been released in the room.

A thin, moaning wail erupted.

The pinpricks of light vanished.

Sabina, listening intently, heard a faint ratchet noise followed by a strumming musical chord. The vaporous light reappeared, now in a different location closer to the floor. At the edge of its glow the guitar could be seen to leap into the air, to gyrate back and forth with no hand upon it. The chord replayed and was joined by others—strange music that sounded as though it were being made by the strings.

For four, five, six seconds the guitar continued its levitating dance, seemingly playing a tune upon itself. Then the glow once more faded, and when it was gone the music ceased and the guitar twanged to rest on the carpet.

What seemed like minutes passed in electric silence.

Grace Cobb suddenly shrieked, "A hand! I felt a hand brush against my cheek!"

Vargas warned, "Do not move, do not break the circle."

Something touched Sabina's neck, a velvety caress that in spite of herself caused a crawling sensation on her scalp. If the fingers—they felt exactly like cold, lifeless fingers—had lingered she would have ignored the professor's remonstration and made an attempt to grab and hold on to them. But the hand or whatever it was slid away almost immediately.

Moments later it materialized just long enough for it to be identifiable as just that, a disembodied hand. Then it was gone as if it had never been there at all.

Another period of breathless silence.

The unearthly moan again.

And a glowing face appeared, as disembodied as the hand, above where Dr. Cobb sat.

The face was a woman's, shrouded as if bound in transparent white drapery cut off in a straight line below the chin. The eyes were enormous black holes. The mouth moved, formed words in a deep-throated rumble.

"Oliver? It is I, Oliver, my son."

"Mother! Oh, I'm so glad you've come at long last." Dr. Cobb's words were choked with feeling. "Are you well, are you content?"

"I am both, yes. But I cannot stay long. The Auras have allowed me to make contact but now I must return."

"So soon? I have so many questions for you . . ."

"And they shall be answered."

"When? When will you come again?"

"Soon. Soon."

"At my next sitting?"

"If the spirits permit. Until then, darling Oliver. Until then . . ."

The face was swallowed by darkness.

More minutes crept away. Sabina couldn't tell how many; she had lost all sense of time and space in the suffocating black.

A second phantomlike countenance materialized then, this one high above Margaret Buckley's chair. It differed from the previous one in that it was smaller, shimmery, and indistinct behind a hazy substance like a luminous veil. The words that issued from it were an otherworldly, childlike quaver—the voice of a little girl.

"Mommy! Is that you, Mommy?"

"Oh, thank heaven. Bernice!" Margaret Buckley's cry was rapturous. "Winthrop, it's our darling Bernice come at last!"

Her husband made no audible response.

"I love you, Mommy. Do you still love me?"

"Oh, yes! Bernice, dearest, I prayed and prayed you'd communicate. Are you happy in the Afterworld? Tell Mommy and Daddy. Daddy's here, too."

"Yes, I know. I love you too, Daddy."

Mr. Buckley was spared having to speak by his wife asking again, "*Are* you happy, darling?"

"Yes, I'm very happy. It's lovely here. But I must go back now."

"No, not yet! Bernice, wait—"

"Will you and Daddy come again, Mommy? Promise me you'll come again. Then the Auras will let me come, too."

"We'll come, I promise! Again and again . . ."

The radiant image vanished.

Mrs. Buckley began to weep softly. The pitiful sound raised Sabina's ire, as it surely did John's. It was despicable enough for predatory, conscienceless men like Abraham Vargas to dupe the gullible, but when they resorted to the exploitation of a mother's yearning for her long-dead child the game was intolerable. The sooner she and John shut down the Unified College of the

Attuned Impulses, the better for everyone. If there was even one more manifestation . . .

There wasn't. She heard scratchings, the unmistakable sound of the slate pencil writing on a slate. This was followed by yet another protracted silence, broken only by the faintest of scraping and clicking sounds that she couldn't identify.

Vargas said abruptly, "The spirits have grown restless. All except Angkar are returning now to their resting places in the land beyond the Border. Angkar will leave too, but first he will free me from my bonds, just as one day we will all be freed from our mortal ties—"

The last word was chopped off in a meaty smacking noise and an explosive grunt of pain. The hand holding Sabina's left hand jerked free. Another smack, then, followed by a brief gurgling moan.

Sabina called out in alarm, "John! Something's happened to Vargas!"

Other voices rose in frightened confusion. As she freed her right hand from Margaret Buckley's grasp and stood up, she heard John's chair scrape backward from the table. It took only scant seconds before his thumbnail scratched a match alight.

In the smoky flare Sabina saw the others rising from their chairs, all except for Vargas. The fake medium, still roped to his armchair, was slumped forward with his chin on his chest, unmoving. John kicked his chair out of the way, carried the upraised match across to the nearest wall sconce. The gas was off; he turned it on and applied the flame. Flickery light burst forth, banishing the darkness.

Outside in the hallway, hands began to beat on the door panel.

Annabelle's voice rose shrilly: "Let me in! I heard a cry from the professor . . . let me in!"

Dr. Cobb had rushed forward and was bending over Vargas. "Dear Lord, he's been stabbed! Stabbed in the back!"

15

QUINCANNON

There were shocked exclamations from the doctor's wife and Winthrop Buckley, overridden by a shriek from Margaret Buckley. Out of the corner of his eye Quincannon saw the woman swoon in her husband's arms as he ran to where Sabina stood staring down at the slumped body in the chair. Her expression of startled incredulity matched that of the others in the room. His own, too, no doubt. This was no piece of mediumistic fakery like the other alleged wonders he'd just witnessed. One look at the dagger jutting from the back of Vargas's neck and the blindly staring eyes made that abundantly clear.

Stabbed, for a fact. And not once but twice. The weapon, whose ornate hilt bore a series of hieroglyphics, had been plunged deep—whether the death blow or a coup de grâce he couldn't tell. The other, first-struck wound, still oozing blood, showed through a rent in Vargas's robe lower down, between the shoulder blades.

Ashen-faced, Dr. Cobb was feeling for a pulse in one limp

wrist. He shook his head and announced unnecessarily, "Expired."

"It isn't possible," Mrs. Cobb whispered in a stricken voice. "How *could* he have been stabbed?"

Buckley had lowered his unconscious wife into one of the chairs and was fanning her flushed face with his hand. He said shakily, "How—and by whom? Surely not any of us . . ."

Quincannon caught Sabina's eye. She wagged her head to tell him she didn't know, or couldn't be sure, what had taken place in those few seconds of darkness.

The psychic assistant, Annabelle, was still beating on the door, clamoring for admittance. Quincannon went to the cabinet. The brass key lay where Vargas had set it down before the séance began; he used it to unlock the door. The woman rushed in from the dark hallway, her eyes wide and fearful. She gave a little moan when she saw Vargas, ran to his side and knelt to peer into his dead face.

When she straightened again her own face looked even more bloodless than before. She said with tremulous outrage, "Which one of you did this?"

"It couldn't have been one of us," Dr. Cobb told her. "No one broke the circle until after the professor was stabbed."

"Then . . . it must have been a malevolent spirit."

Malevolent spirit, Quincannon thought sourly. *Bah!*

"He did perceive antagonistic waves tonight," Cobb said. "But why would such a spirit—?"

"He made the Auras angry at times. I warned him to be more cautious but he wouldn't listen."

Sabina said, "How did he make the Auras angry?"

Annabelle shuddered and shook her head. Then her eyes shifted into a long stare across the room. "The slates," she said.

"What about the slates?"

"Is there a spirit message? Have you looked?"

Quincannon swung around to the cabinet; the others, except for Margaret Buckley, crowded close behind him. The tied slates were in the center of the stack where Vargas had placed them. He left those two out, undid the knot in his handkerchief, parted the slates and held them up side by side.

Murmurs, and a mildly blasphemous exclamation from Buckley.

In a ghostlike hand beneath the "John Milford" signatures on each, one message upside down and backward as if it were a mirror image of the other, was written: *I Angkar destroyed the offensive one.*

"Angkar!" Cobb said. "Why would the professor's guide and guardian turn on him in such a terrible way?"

"The spirits are not mocked," Annabelle said. "They know wickedness when it is done in their name. Guardian then becomes avenger."

"Madam, what are you saying?"

"I warned him," she said again. "He would not listen and now he has paid the price. His torment will continue on the Other Side, until his spirit has been cleansed of all wickedness."

Quincannon had had all he could stand of this nonsense. He said, "Enough talk and speculation," in a sharp authoritarian voice that swiveled all heads in his direction. "There will be time for that later. Now there's work to be done."

"Quite right," Cobb agreed. "The police—"

"Not the police, Doctor. Not yet."

"Here, Mr. Milford, who are you to take charge?"

"The name isn't Milford, it's Quincannon. John Quincannon. Of Carpenter and Quincannon, Professional Detective Services."

Cobb gaped at him. "A detective? You?"

"Two detectives." He gestured to Sabina at his side. "My partner, Mrs. Carpenter."

"A *woman*?" Grace Cobb said. She sounded as shocked as if Sabina had been revealed as a soiled dove.

Sabina, testily: "And why not, pray tell?"

Annabelle, angrily: "Blasphemy! The presence of unbelievers served only to increase the wrath of the spirits."

Dr. Cobb: "Who hired you? Who brought you here under false pretenses?"

Quincannon and Sabina both looked at Buckley. To the man's credit, he wasted no time in admitting he was their client.

"You, Winthrop?" Margaret Buckley had revived and was regarding them dazedly. "I don't understand. Why would you engage detectives?"

Before her husband could reply, Quincannon said, "Mr. Buckley will explain in the parlor. Be so good, all of you, as to go there and wait."

"For what?" Cobb demanded.

"For Mrs. Carpenter and myself to do what no other detective, police officer, or private citizen can do half so well. Solve a baffling crime."

No one protested, although Dr. Cobb wore an expression of disapproval and Annabelle said, "What good are earthly detectives when it is the spirits who have taken vengeance?" as they left the séance room. Within a minute Quincannon and Sabina were alone with the dead man. He turned the key in the lock to ensure their privacy.

"Murder," she said, shaking her head. "That is the last thing I expected to happen tonight. And in such a bizarre fashion, in total darkness."

"Indeed. A pretty puzzle, eh?"

"Mm." She straightened her shoulders. The events had unnerved her initially, but she was never unflappable for long. Nor squeamish in the presence of violent death. "Now we'll see if we can make good on your boast."

They proceeded, first extinguishing the incense burner and opening one of the locked windows so that cold night air could refresh the room. Then they carefully examined walls, fireplace, and floor. All were solid; there were no secret openings, crawlspaces, hidey-holes, or trapdoors. Quincannon then went to inspect the corpse, while Sabina gave her attention to the jar-encased bell on the table.

The first thing he noticed was that although the rope still bound Vargas to his chair, it was somewhat loose across forearms and sternum. When he lifted the limp left hand he found that it had been freed of the bonds. The right foot had also been freed. Confirmation of his suspicions in both cases. His next discovery was also more or less expected: the two items concealed inside the sleeve of the medium's robe.

He was studying these when Sabina said, "No surprise here. The jar was fastened to the tabletop with gum adhesive to hold it in place during the tipping business."

"Can you pry it loose?"

"I already have. The clapper on the bell—"

"Is either missing or frozen. Eh?"

"Frozen. Vargas used another bell to produce his spirit rings."

"This one." Quincannon held up the tiny hand bell with its gauze-muffled clapper. "Made and struck so as to produce a hollow ring, as if it were coming from the bell inside the jar. The directionless quality of sounds in total darkness, and the power of suggestion, completed the deception."

"All just as Madame Louella explained the trick. What else have you there?"

He showed her the second item from Vargas's sleeve.

"A reaching rod," she said. "Mmm, yes."

Quincannon said, "His right hand was holding your left wrist on the table. Could you tell when he freed it?"

"No, and I was waiting for it to happen. I think he may have done it when he coughed. You recall?"

"I do."

"He must have practiced that bit of deception hundreds of times in order to perfect it," Sabina said. "Quite cunning in his warped way."

"And now quite dead."

"Have you a suggestion as to who stabbed him?"

"Not as yet, except that it wasn't the fictitious Angkar or any other supernatural agency. Annabelle may believe in spirits who wield daggers, but I don't."

"Nor I. I suppose our client could be responsible—he made no bones about his anger toward Vargas when I last spoke to him in his office—but he doesn't seem the type of man to resort to violence, particularly not in circumstances such as these."

"We don't know him well enough to discount hidden depths," Quincannon pointed out. "Nor the Cobbs. You noticed the way Mrs. Cobb petted Vargas in the parlor earlier?"

"And the look that passed between them, yes. I expect Dr. Cobb noticed it, too. Jealousy is a strong motive for murder, the more so if there was infidelity involved."

"A woman scorned is another strong motive."

Sabina nodded. "Annabelle would also qualify in both cases," she said. "Except that she wasn't in the room when Vargas was stabbed and the door was securely locked. The guilty person must be one of the four at the table."

"So it would seem. One clever enough to break the circle in the same way Vargas did and then to stand up, commit the deed, and return to his chair—all in utter darkness."

"Doesn't seem possible, does it."

Quincannon said, "No more impossible than any of the other humbug we witnessed tonight."

"True. This isn't the first such enigma we've encountered."

"Indeed. We already have some of the answers to the evening's queer show. Find the rest and I'll soon have the solution to the riddle of Vargas's death."

"*We'll* soon have the solution, you mean."

He knew better than to argue the point.

One of the missing answers came from an examination of the dead man's mystic rings. The one on his left hand that Sabina said he'd referred to as an Egyptian signet and seal talisman ring had a hidden fingernail catch; when it was flipped, the entire top hinged upward to reveal a small sturdy hook within. Quincannon had no doubt that were he to drop down on all fours and peer under the table in front of Vargas's chair, he would find a tiny metal eye screwed to the wood.

The miraculous self-playing guitar, which of course was nothing of the kind, drew him next. He already knew how its dancing levitation had been managed; a close scrutiny of the instrument revealed the rest of the trick.

"John, look at this."

Sabina was at the cabinet, fingering a small bottle. When he'd set the guitar down and joined her, he saw that she had removed the bottle's glass stopper. "This was among the others on the tray," she told him, and held it up for him to sniff its contents.

"Ah," he said. "Almond oil."

"Mixed with white phosphorous, no doubt."

"The contents of the other bottles?"

"Liquor and incense oils. Nothing more than window dressing."

Quincannon stood looking at the cabinet. At length he knelt and ran his fingers over its smooth front, its fancily inlayed center top. There seemed to be neither doors nor a way to lift open the top, as if the cabinet might be a sealed wooden box. This proved not to be the case. It took him a few minutes to locate the secret spring catch, cleverly concealed as it was among the dark-squared inlays. As soon as he pressed it, the catch released noiselessly and the entire top slid up and back on oiled hinges.

The interior was a narrow, hollow space—a box, in fact, that seemed more like a child's toy chest than a cabinet. A clutch of items were pushed into one corner. Quincannon lifted them out one by one.

More than a yard of white silk.

Another yard of fine white netting, so fine that it could be wadded into a ball no larger than a walnut.

A two-foot-square piece of black cloth.

A small container of safety matches.

A theatrical mask.

And a pair of rubber gloves almost but not quite identical, both of which had been stuffed with cotton and dipped in melted paraffin.

He returned each item to the cabinet, finally closed the lid. He said with satisfaction, "That leaves only the writing on the slates. And we know how that was done, don't we, my dear."

"We also know now how Vargas was murdered," Sabina said. "And by whom. Don't we, my dear."

Quincannon elevated an eyebrow. "You have the answer, too?"

"Naturally. Did you really believe you're the only one of us adept at solving seemingly impossible crimes?"

16

SABINA

Neither Winthrop Buckley nor the Cobbs took kindly to being ushered back into the séance room, even though John had moved Vargas's body and chair away from the table and covered them with one of the window drapes. There was some grumbling when he asked the couples to assume their former positions around the table, but they all complied. A seventh chair had been added at Vargas's place; he invited Annabelle to sit there. She, too, complied, maintaining a stoic silence.

Buckley appealed to Sabina. "Will this take long? My wife has borne the worst of this ordeal. She isn't well."

This was evident from Margaret Buckley's talcumlike pallor, the slump of her shoulders, and her somewhat blank stare—the tragic look of a woman suffering from the shattering of hopes and beliefs. Sabina said, "Not long, Mr. Buckley, I assure you."

"Is it absolutely necessary for us to be in here?"

"It is, for reasons which will become apparent."

John looked around at the others. "We have nothing to fear from the dead, past or present," he said. "Spirits were not responsible for what took place during the séance. Not any of it."

Grace Cobb: "Are you implying one of us stabbed poor Professor Vargas?"

"I am."

Annabelle: "No, you're wrong. It was Angkar, just as he wrote on the slate. You must not deny the spirits. The penalties—"

"A pox on the penalties," John said. "Vargas was murdered by a living, flesh-and-blood person."

Dr. Cobb: "Who? If you're so all-fired certain it was one of us, name him."

"Perhaps it was you, Doctor."

"See here—! What motive could I possibly have?"

"Any one of several. Such as discovery prior to tonight that your trusted medium was a fake—"

"A fake!"

"—and you were so enraged that you sought to put a permanent end to his nefarious activities."

"Preposterous."

John's flair for the dramatic was at the fore now. That was apparent to Sabina from the glint in his eye and the swell of his breast. She would put up with it for a time, but not throughout this interrogation. It was she whom Winthrop Buckley had hired, her investigative work that had confirmed Vargas's charlatanism, her deductions about the murder the equal of his, and she was not about to allow him to claim all the credit for himself.

He had turned his gaze on Grace Cobb. "The same could be true of you, Mrs. Cobb. Perhaps you're the guilty party."

She regarded him haughtily. "If that is an accusation—"

"Not at all. Merely a suggestion of possibility, of hidden motives of your own regarding your relationship with the deceased."

"I had no relationship with Professor Vargas. None whatsoever!" Which may or may not have been the truth, though the faint flush on Grace Cobb's cheeks indicated that it wasn't.

"Or it could be you, Mr. Buckley," John said, "and your having engaged the services of our agency a smokescreen to hide your lethal intentions for the evening."

The investor's eyes, magnified by his spectacles, glittered with anger. And rightly so. Sabina said warningly, "That'll do, John."

"It had better do," the investor said, "if you entertain any hope of receiving the balance of your fee. You know full well neither I nor my wife ended that scoundrel's life."

Dr. Cobb: "I don't see how it could possibly have been any of us. We were all seated here—all except Annabelle who was on the other side of the locked door. And none of us broke the mystic circle."

"Are you certain of that, Doctor?"

"Of course I'm certain."

"But you're wrong. Vargas himself broke it."

"He couldn't have, it wasn't possible—"

"Not only possible, but relatively easy to manage."

"Why would he do such a thing? For an entranced medium to break the mystic circle is to risk the wrath of the spirits, endanger his own life. He told us so himself."

"He had already incurred the wrath of the all-powerful Auras," Annabelle said fervidly. "It was Angkar, I tell you. Angkar who plunged the dagger into his body."

John ignored her. He said to no one in particular, "You don't seem to have grasped my words to you a minute ago. Professor Vargas was a fake. The Unified College of the Attuned Impulses is a fake. He was no more sensitive to the spirit world than you or I or President Cleveland."

Margaret Buckley emitted a whimpering sound. Her face was strained, her eyes feverish. "That . . . that can't be true! Everything we saw and heard tonight . . . the visitations . . . my daughter . . ."

"Sham and illusion, the lot of it," Sabina said gently. "I am very sorry, Mrs. Buckley."

"I don't believe it, it couldn't be . . ."

"Mrs. Carpenter and I will prove it to you, madam," John said, "by explaining all of Vargas's tricks during the séance. To begin with, the way in which he freed his right hand while seeming to maintain an unbroken clasp with Mrs. Carpenter's." He fluffed his beard and drew a long, slow breath, preparatory to beginning to orate.

Sabina was not about to allow him to hog center stage. She spoke quickly before he could. "The essence of that trick lies in the fact that the hand consists of both a wrist and fingers and the wrist is able to bend in different directions. The fingers of Vargas's right hand were gripping my wrist, Mrs. Cobb's fingers gripping his left wrist. By maneuvering his hands closer and closer together as he talked, in a series of tiny movements, he also brought our hands closer together. When they were near enough for his thumbs to touch, he freed his right hand in one quick movement and immediately reestablished control of my wrist with his other hand, the one whose wrist was being held by Mrs. Cobb."

Mr. Buckley: "But how could he manage that when we were all concentrating on tight control?"

"He coughed once, rather loudly, if you recall. The sound was a calculated aural distraction. In that instant—and an instant was all it took—he completed the maneuver. He also relied on the fact that a person's senses become unreliable after a protracted period of sitting in total darkness. What you think you see, hear, feel at any given moment may in fact be partly or completely erroneous."

During a brief silence while the others digested this, John cast a frowning look at Sabina. She wrinkled her nose at him.

Dr. Cobb said, "Even with one hand free, how could he have rung the spirit bell? I bound him myself, as you saw, and I am morally certain the loops and knots were tight."

"You may be certain in your own mind, Doctor," Sabina told him, "but the facts are otherwise. It is a virtual impossibility for anyone to securely bind a person to a chair with a single length of rope. And you were flurried, self-conscious, anxious to acquit yourself well of the business, and you are a gentleman besides. You would hardly bind a man such as Professor Vargas, whom you admired and respected, with enough constriction of the rope to cut into his flesh and affect his circulation. A fraction of an inch of slack is all a man who has been tied many times before, who is skilled in muscular control, requires in order to free one hand."

Dr. Cobb was unable to refute the logic of this. He lapsed into a somewhat daunted silence as Sabina went on to explain and demonstrate the bell-ringing trick.

"Next," she said when she'd finished, "we have the table

tipping and levitation. Vargas accomplished this phenomenon with but one hand and one foot, the left lower extremity having been freed with the aid of the upper right. He—"

John interrupted her by holding up the Egyptian talisman ring, which he had removed from Vargas's finger, and releasing the fingernail catch to reveal the hook within. "He attached this hook to a small eye screwed beneath the table, after which he gave a sharp upward tug. The table legs on his end were lifted off the carpet just far enough for him to slip the toe of his shoe under one leg, thus creating a 'human clamp' which gave him full control of the table. By lifting his ring and elevating his toe while the heel remained on the carpet, he was able to make the table tilt, rock, gyrate at will."

Sabina added quickly, before John could continue, "And when he was ready for the table to appear to levitate, he simply unhooked his ring and thrust upward with his foot, withdrawing it immediately afterward. The illusion of the table seeming to float under our hands for a second or two before it fell was enhanced by the circumstances and the darkness."

Buckley, with some bitterness: "It all seems so blasted obvious when explained."

"Such flummery always is, Mr. Buckley. It is the trappings and manipulation that make it mystifying. The so-called spirit lights are another example." Sabina placed the stoppered glass bottle on the table and described where she'd found it and what it contained. "Mix white phosphorous with any fatty oil, and the result is a bottle filled with hidden light. As long as the bottle remains stoppered the phosphorous gives off no glow, but as soon as the cork is removed and air is permitted to reach the mixture, a faint unearthly shine results. Wave the bottle in the air and the light seems to dart about. Replace the stopper and the light fades away as the air inside is used up."

"The little winking lights were more of the same, I suppose?"

"Not quite," John said. "Match heads were their source. Hold a match head between the moistened forefinger and thumb of each hand, wiggle the forefinger enough to expose and then once more quickly conceal the match head, and you have flitting fireflies."

Grace Cobb asked, "The guitar that seemed to dance and play itself—how was that done?"

John fetched the guitar, brought it back to the table. Beside it he set the reaching rod from Vargas's sleeve. The rod was only a few inches in length when closed, but when he opened out each of its sections after the fashion of a telescope, it extended the full length of the table and beyond—more than six feet overall.

"Vargas extended this rod in his left hand," he said, "inserted it in the hole in the neck of the guitar, raised and slowly turned the instrument this way and that to create the illusion of air-dancing. As for the music . . ."

He reached into the oval sound hole under the strings, gave a quick twist. The weird strumming they had heard during the séance began to emanate from within.

Mrs. Cobb: "A music box!"

"A one-tune music box, to be precise," Sabina said, "affixed to the wood inside with gum adhesive."

Mr. Buckley: "The hand that touched Mrs. Cobb's cheek? The manifestations? The spirit writing on the slate?"

"All part and parcel of the same trickery," John told him. Again he went to the cabinet, where he pressed the hidden release to raise its top. From inside he took out the two stuffed and wax-coated rubber gloves, held them up. "These are the ghostly 'fingers' that touched Mrs. Cobb and Mrs. Carpenter. The smoothness of the paraffin gives them the feel of human flesh. One 'hand' has been treated with luminous paint; it was kept covered under this"—he showed them the black cloth—"until the time came to reveal it as a glowing disembodied entity."

He lifted out the silk drapery and theatrical mask. "The mask has been treated in the same fashion. It was the combination of these two items that created the manifestation alleged to be Dr. Cobb's mother."

He raised the fine white netting. "Likewise made phosphorescent and draped over the head to create the 'spirit' purported to be the Buckleys' daughter."

"But . . . I heard Bernice speak," Margaret Buckley said weakly. "It was her voice, I'm sure it was . . ."

Her husband took her hand in both of us. "No, my dear, it wasn't. You only imagined it to be."

"An imitation of a child's voice," Sabina said, "just as the other voice was an imitation of a man's deep articulation."

John picked up the two slates, which bore the "spirit message" under his false signatures. "*I Angkar destroyed the evil one.* The actual murderer wrote those words, in sequence on one slate and upside down and backward on the other to heighten the illusion of spirit writing. *Before* the crime was committed, in anticipation of it."

"Who?" Dr. Cobb demanded. "Name the person, sir."

"Professor Vargas's accomplice, of course."

"Accomplice?"

Once again Sabina spoke before John could. "No one individual, no matter how skilled in supernatural fakery, could have arranged and carried out all the tricks we were subjected to even if he *hadn't* been roped to his chair. Someone else had to direct the reaching rod to the guitar and then turn the spring on the music box. Someone else had to jangle the tambourine, make the wailing noises, carry the phosphorous bottle to different parts of the room and up onto the love seat there so as to make the light seem to float near the ceiling. Someone else had to manipulate the waxed gloves, don the mask and drapery and netting, imitate the spirit voices."

"Annabelle? Are you saying it was Annabelle?"

"None other."

They all stared at the silent, black-robed woman at the head of the table. Her expression remained frozen, but her eyes burned with a zealot's fire.

Dr. Cobb said, "But she wasn't in the room with us . . ."

"Ah, but she was," John said quickly. "At first it seemed to me that she must be in another part of the house—"

"Seemed to *us*," Sabina corrected him with a touch of asperity. Then to the others, "Not because of the locked door but because of the way in which the lights dimmed and then extinguished to begin the séance. As though she turned off the gas at a prearranged time. But that wasn't the case. Some type of automatic timing mechanism was used for that purpose. Annabelle, you see, was already present in this room before the rest of us entered and Vargas locked the door."

Mr. Buckley: "Before, you say?"

"She disappeared from the parlor, you'll recall, as soon as she announced that all was in readiness. While Vargas detained us with his call for 'donations,' Annabelle shed her robe and slipped in here—"

Dr. Cobb: "Shed her robe?"

"Yes, certainly. It would have been too cumbersome for the performance of all the necessary tricks in the dark, might possibly have made rustling sounds that would have given her away. Whereas dressed only in some sort of close-fitting, black undergarment she had complete freedom of movement. Such also made it easier for her to conceal herself before and after the commission of her crime."

"Conceal herself where? There are no hiding places . . . unless you expect us to believe she crawled up inside the fireplace chimney."

"Not there, no. Nor are there any secret closets or the like. She was hidden in the same place as her spirit props, *within the cabinet*. The interior is hollow, and she is both tiny and enough of a practiced contortionist to fold her body into such a short, narrow space."

"The catch that releases the hinged top," John said, reclaiming the narrative, "can be operated from within as well. Once the room was in total darkness and Vargas began invoking the spirits, she climbed out to commence her preparations. Gloves and a mask to cover her white face completed her all-black costume. And her familiarity with the room allowed her to move about in silence."

"All well and good," Mr. Buckley said, "but the woman was

outside the locked door, pounding on it, less than a minute after Vargas was stabbed. Explain that."

"Simple misdirection, sir. Before the stabbing she replaced all props inside the cabinet and closed the top, then unlocked the door; the key, despite careful oiling of the keyhole, made a faint scraping and the bolt likewise clicked slightly as it released—sounds which I . . . which Mrs. Carpenter and I both heard. Annabelle then crossed the room, plunged her dagger into Vargas's back and neck, recrossed the room after the second thrust, let herself out into the darkened hallway, and relocked the door from that side. Not with Vargas's key, which remained on the cabinet, but with a duplicate key of her own."

No one spoke for a cluster of seconds. In hushed tones, then, Margaret Buckley asked, "Why, Annabelle? Why did you do it?"

The woman's mouth twisted. Her voice, when it came, was fiery with passion and more than a hint of madness. "He was evil, an unbeliever, a fornicator. He mocked the spirits with his schemes, laughed and derided them and those of us who truly believe. I did his bidding because I loved him, I obeyed him and overlooked his wantonness until two nights ago when the spirits came to me and whispered that I must obey and overlook no longer. They told me I must destroy him, and to do so during one of his false séances. A powerful spirit from the highest plane in the Afterworld, not the pretend one called Angkar, guided my hand tonight. It showed me the path to the truth and light of the Auras . . ."

Her words trailed off; she sat staring fixedly. Her blazing eyes looked at no one in this room, Sabina thought, but at whatever she believed waited for her beyond the veil.

17

QUINCANNON

It was after midnight before the bumbling constabulary (he considered all but a handful of city policemen to be bumbling) finished with their questions, took Annabelle and the remains of A. Vargas away, and permitted the others to depart.

Fortunately the homicide detective in charge was a man Quincannon knew only slightly and who had no ax to grind with him. If the dick in charge had been the beefy, red-faced, and doubtless corrupt Prussian, Kleinhoffer, the interrogation would not have gone half as smoothly. Each rubbed the other the wrong way, a mutual antipathy that had led to clashes in the past.

After helping his wife into their phaeton, Winthrop Buckley drew Quincannon and Sabina aside. He said to her, "You and your partner are competent detectives, Mrs. Carpenter, I'll grant you that even though I don't entirely approve of your methods."

"I only wish your wife had been spared the horror of Vargas's murder."

"As do I. But I have a feeling that once she recovers, she will abandon her faith in mediums and her quest for an audience with our daughter's spirit."

"I hope so, Mr. Buckley."

Quincannon said, "If you should find yourself in need of our services again, sir . . ."

"I trust I won't. One question before we part. As I told Mrs. Carpenter at our first meeting, the first séance we attended here was concluded by Vargas's claim that Angkar had untied him. We heard the rope flung through the air, and when the gas was turned up we saw it lying unknotted on the floor. He couldn't have untied all those knots himself, with only one hand. How was that trick done?"

"Annabelle assisted in it, too. The unknotted rope, which he himself hurled across the room, was not the same one with which he was tied. In the darkness she slipped up behind him and cut the knotted rope into pieces with her dagger, then hid the pieces in the cabinet. The second rope was concealed there with the other props and given to Vargas after she'd severed the first."

"His planned finale for tonight's séance as well, I expect."

"No doubt."

Buckley shook Sabina's hand, then Quincannon's. "We'll be leaving now. I would offer you both a ride, but there is hardly enough room for two more passengers. And Margaret is in no condition for any more company."

"We wouldn't trouble you in any event," Sabina said. "Dr. Cobb has offered to take us to the nearest cab stand."

The short ride in the Cobbs' roomy landau to Market and Van Ness, where the nearest stand was located, was conducted in silence. Grace Cobb sat hunched in the passenger side corner, arms folded across her breast, her blond head bowed; she had hardly spoken since the explanations in the spirit room, had in fact remained mostly silent from the time Vargas's body was discovered. In light of Annabelle's revelation that Vargas had been a fornicator, Quincannon suspected that she and the fake medium had been more than just business acquaintances. Whether Dr. Cobb's reticence was the result of a similar suspicion, or merely a delayed reaction to the evening's events, was none of his business.

Sabina, too, had nothing to say in the Cobbs' presence or in the hansom on the way to her Russian Hill flat. Nor did she sit any closer to Quincannon than Grace Cobb had to her husband in the landau. She seemed peeved at him for some reason he couldn't fathom. Finally, halfway through the ride, he broached the question to her.

"You know the answer, John," she said. "Don't be obtuse."

"Obtuse? What have I done?"

"The Buckley investigation was mine to begin with, the explanations to the spiritualist trickery largely the result of my conference with Madame Louella, and the solution to Vargas's untimely demise as much mine as it was yours."

"I don't dispute that, my dear—"

"But you saw fit as usual to claim all the credit."

"I did no such thing—"

"Yes you did. You and your dratted flair for the dramatic. If I hadn't kept interrupting, you would have rattled on through the entire set of explanations without letting me put a word in edgewise."

Quincannon was honestly surprised. "But I had no intention of shutting you out. If I spoke too quickly and too often, it was purely unintentional—"

"Oh, bosh. You're worse than a ward politician when it comes to self-serving oratory."

"Self-serving? That's not true."

"It is true. You fancy yourself a master detective without equal and you seize every opportunity to prove it to the world. Well, you're not without equal, John Quincannon, whether you believe it or not."

"But you know how much I respect your ability—"

"Respect it but consider it inferior to yours. Well, it's not. I am just as adept as you at solving difficult cases, and that includes your specialty of seemingly impossible crimes. And you know it whether you admit it or not."

"I do admit it. Haven't I said so to you more than once?"

"Saying and believing are two different things."

"I do not consider you inferior," he said. "Truly, honestly."

"Well, you certainly acted like it tonight."

Quincannon was somewhat cowed. "I didn't mean to be insensitive, didn't realize I was deprecating you in any way. I apologize. Nothing like it will ever happen again."

"So you say now."

"A solemn promise, my dear."

"You had better mean it."

"I do, I swear it." He reached over, tentatively closed his fingers around her hand. For a moment he thought she would pull hers away, but she didn't. "Am I forgiven?"

"You're forgiven. Provisionally."

They sat once more in silence, companionably now, the stillness broken only by the jangle of the horse's bit chains, the clatter of the cab's iron wheels on the cobblestones. Yes, Quincannon thought, he had learned Sabina's lesson well. He would no longer indulge his passion for the limelight, the approbation of others at his prowess.

Not while she was involved and present, ever again.

Sunday was a quiet day.

Quincannon would have liked to spend it with Sabina, but she had a date to go riding in the park with her friend Amity Wellman and other members of the Golden Gate Ladies Bicycle Club. Dinner with her was not possible, either. After the day's bicycling, there was a meeting at the Wellman home of Voting Rights for Women, of which Amity was head and Sabina an ardent member, in preparation for the California State Woman Suffrage Convention next month.

He slept late, catching up on the past week's lost sleep, then rode a trolley car to the Cobweb Palace, Abe Warner's eccentric eatery on Meigg's Wharf, for a leisurely meal of abalone steak and rhubarb pie. One of two slumming young women at a nearby table kept casting glances in his direction and smiling when she caught his eye. Interested and flirtatious—a sort he knew well from past experience. It would have been easy enough to have made her acquaintance, and eventually if not immediately been permitted to sample her favors.

But now, feeling as he did about Sabina, he was not even slightly tempted. There was something a bit sad in that, in the transformation . . . no, the demise . . . of a practiced ladies' man. Not that he regretted it. A woman as attractive, as exciting, as exceptional as Sabina made all others seem deficient in both charm and sex appeal.

After lunch he went for a stroll through the Sunday bazaar in the open field opposite the Palace Hotel, with its salmagundi of patent medicine and physical therapy pitchmen, phrenologists, palm readers, temperance speakers, organ grinders, food sellers, Salvation Army musicians. He viewed all of this with his usual jaundiced eye, stopping at none of the booths and buying nothing, but it helped pass the afternoon.

A light evening meal and games of pool and snooker, both of which he played expertly, at Hoolihan's Saloon, and then home to his lonely flat to read from his collection of volumes of poetry until it was time for bed. All in all a pleasant enough Sunday.

But it would have been so much better had he shared it with Sabina.

18

QUINCANNON

Monday, like Sunday, was another uneventful day. Or it was until that evening.

He heard nothing from Ezra Bluefield or any of his other contacts regarding the coney game, there was no old business that required his attention nor any new business at all. The only thing that made it tolerable was Sabina's presence in the office, and at that she refused to allow him to do nothing more than sit at his desk smoking his pipe and meditating; instead she coerced him into helping her with billing matters and the updating of the agency's file of dossiers on known criminals. Paperwork, bah! He was a man of action, when there was any action to be had, not a glorified clerk.

He made the mistake of saying that last to Sabina, and received a tongue-lashing in return. "Is that what you think *I* am, a glorified clerk?" she said crossly.

"No, no, of course not . . ."

"I do most of the invoicing and bill-paying, as you well know. Not to mention writing reports, handling our finances, and now and then conducting an investigation such as the one for Winthrop Buckley. And yet you growl and grumble every time I ask you to do a few simple tasks to ease my burden, even when you're not busy."

Quincannon swallowed a sigh. A small crisis last night, and now another today. Women could be difficult on occasion, an emancipated woman twofold. Not that he blamed her for pointing out what few shortcomings he possessed. She did spend a great deal of her time attending to office chores he avoided, and clearly found them as dull and repetitious as he did.

He poured oil on the troubled waters by saying, "You're right, my dear, and you'll get no more argument from me. What would you like me to do?"

"Write the report on the Buckley case. I'll give you my notes."

And a long, detailed report it was bound to be. Ah, well. He tackled it with as much good humor as he could muster. He made sure to give most of the credit for the investigation's successful resolution to Sabina—she deserved it, after all—and to minimize his own role in the matter. When he showed the finished report to her and she'd read through it, she nodded and smiled her approval.

"Now that wasn't such a difficult chore, was it, John?"

"Not at all."

The white lie earned him another smile, a warmer one to show that he was back in her good graces.

The rest of the day crawled away. The prospect of an intimate dinner for two would have made the slow passage of time more tolerable, but he'd been thwarted once again by her involvement with the suffrage movement: she was dining tonight with her cousin Callie French and other female members of the social set in an effort to raise more funding for the upcoming convention. Another dull evening loomed ahead for him.

Sabina departed early and Quincannon closed the office shortly afterward. *Home? No, Hoolihan's.* There, at least, he would have the company of other lonely souls in a convivial atmosphere.

Hoolihan's Saloon was a haven for those who disliked the noisy grandiosity of the tony saloons that catered to the politicians, judges, businessmen, and prowling gay blades who indulged in the nightly Cocktail Route bacchanal. Small merchants, office workers, tradesmen, Embarcadero dock-wallopers were its clientele—men who preferred a place free of the glitter of crystal chandeliers and fancy mirrors, a floor coated with sawdust, a back room packed with pool, billiard, and snooker tables, and a stomach-filling free repast of corned beef, strong cheese, rye bread, pigs' feet, hard-boiled eggs, and pickles. Some were solitary drinkers, whose privacy was respected by staff and patrons alike. Quincannon had been drawn there in his drinking days, and even after taking the pledge continued to frequent it. He knew most of the regulars well and considered the head bartender, Ben Joyce, a friend.

"Hello, you bloody Scotsman," Joyce said, his usual greeting, when Quincannon bellied up. "Back again tonight, eh?"

"In spite of having to look at your ugly face."

"Hah. At least mine doesn't resemble a black sheep's hind end."

He poured a mug of warm clam juice without being asked, set it in front of Quincannon with a feigned expression of distaste. "Only a barbarian would drink the likes of this," he said.

"You must have a fair lot of barbarians among your customers, else you wouldn't stock it."

Quincannon had been there for the better part of half an hour, and was helping himself to a generous plate of free food, when a little, seedy-looking fellow in a patched coat and lye-colored pants sidled up to him and tugged on his sleeve. No one he'd ever seen before, and not the sort to be drawn to or long tolerated in Hoolihan's at any rate, dressed as he was and giving off a ripe odor of unwashed flesh.

"You be Mr. Quincannon, eh?" he said in a voice like a frog's croak. An Australian frog, judging from the slight accent. Like as not a second-generation Sydney Duck.

"And if I am?"

"I was told I might find you here. Me name's Owney."

Quincannon extricated his sleeve from the grubby fingers. "What do you want?"

"A private word with you, sir, to your benefit."

"Who told you to look me up?"

"A gent I knows gives me your name. An acquaintance, as you might say, of Mr. Ezra Bluefield."

Quincannon's interest sharpened considerably at the mention of Bluefield's name. "Come along, then," he said. "We'll have our private word at one of the tables."

Owney was eyeing the plate of food, his tongue flicking over chapped lips; obviously it was much more appetizing fare than he was used to. "Would you mind, sir, if I was to have a bite to eat meself? Pigs' feet's always been me favorite."

"We'll talk first. If what you have to say is worthwhile, you can have this plateful."

"And p'raps a glass of beer to quench me thirst?"

"That, too."

"Ah, I can tell you're a gentleman, sir, a true gentlemen. You'll not be disappointed in what I haves to tell you, I guarantee it."

Quincannon steered him to an empty corner table near the window, set the plate down in the middle of it. Owney started to sit down beside him, but Quincannon waved him to a chair opposite. The ripe body odor was not quite as palpably offensive at a distance.

"Speak your piece," he said then.

"Well, sir, I gets around a bit and keeps me ears open. Couple of nights ago I happens to be in a Terrific Street resort and overhears a mug in his cups tell another mug how happy he was to've hooked up with them that was takin' the Treasury Department for a ride. His exact words, sir. So when I hears that a pal of Mr. Bluefield's is interested in just such dirty business as that, I comes lookin' for you straightaway."

"What else was said on the subject?"

"Nothing that I hears. The second mug says hard, 'Shut up, Dinger, or the boss'll cut your tongue out.'"

"Dinger. You're sure that was the name?"

"That I am, sir. No mistake."

"Was the boss's name mentioned? Or any others?"

"Dinger was all I hears."

"Any idea where Dinger or the other one hang their hats?"

"No, sir. Strangers to me, they was."

"Where was it you overheard them talking?"

"The Red Rooster. You knows it, sir?"

"I know it," Quincannon said. The Red Rooster was a dance hall and bagnio on Terrific Street, as Pacific Avenue was known to habitués, in the black heart of the Barbary Coast. "Was anyone else with the pair while they were talking?"

"Not then there wasn't, but one of the girls joined them up just after. Joined Dinger up, that is." Owney punctuated the last with a wink and a leer. "Wasn't long before they goes wobblin' off together, headed upstairs."

"No stranger to him, then, this girl?"

"Chummy as you please, they was."

"Do you know her name?"

"Mollie. That's what he called her."

"What does she look like?"

"Hefty as them that likes 'em that way. Ringlets what fits right in with the name of the place, red as a rooster's comb."

"And Dinger?"

"Well, now. A mite taller than me, speckled-egg bald without his hat. Nose bent funny, like it was broke once and not fixed proper. Fond of his liquor, I'd say—face as red as Mollie's hair."

"Age?"

"Who can tell, sir? Not so old, not so young."

"The other man, the one who told Dinger to shut up—describe him."

"Shaped like a wrestler, he was, with a mustache so thick it looked like he was eating a cat."

Paddy Lasher, like as not. "Did you notice his eyes, if one was blue and the other brown?"

"Hoo. One blue, one brown? No, sir." Owney gave an emphatic headshake. "I never looks them in the eye as I don't know, and even if I did, the Rooster ain't too well lit up like some resorts."

"Anything else you can tell me about either man?"

"Not a thing, sir. If I'd knowed then what I knows now, I'd've waited around and followed Dinger and his pal when they left the Rooster. As 'twas, I had some business of me own to tend to."

Scruff's business, no doubt. Men like Owney had their fingers in the bottoms of all sorts of unsavory barrels.

Owney leaned forward, his gaze shifting eagerly between Quincannon and the plate full of free lunch. "Was me information worth this here tucker for a hungry man?"

Quincannon pushed the plate toward him.

"And a glass to wash it down with?"

"Yes."

"Ah. And not to be askin' too much of your charity, sir, pr'aps a gold sovereign or two for me empty purse?"

The idea of paying money to a scruff as disreputable as this one, particularly when there was no chance of an expense-account reimbursement, chafed at Quincannon's sense of propriety, not to mention his thrifty nature. A promise, however, was a promise. He got to his feet, withdrew a handful of coins from his pocket, extracted two dimes, and placed them on the table.

"One for the promised beer," he said, "the other for your empty purse."

Owney looked half crestfallen, half irritated, but he knew better than to offer a remark. He pounced on the coins, made them disappear. When last seen he had a pig's foot in one hand and a hunk of cheese in the other and was greedily devouring them in alternate bites.

19

QUINCANNON

He seldom ventured into the nine-square-block lair of the Barbary Coast after nightfall. But when business demanded it, he didn't think twice about assuming the risk. The lead provided by Owney struck him as genuine, made him eager to find Dinger and his "cat-eating" friend. And even more eager to learn the identity of "the boss." He'd like nothing better than another confrontation with Long Nick Darrow, if Darrow was in fact alive and practicing his trade again after ten long years. Should the boss be someone else, how he'd been able to utilize Darrow's special counterfeiting skills was an equally burning question that compelled an answer.

Before he went on the hunt, Quincannon stopped at the agency. To go traipsing around the Coast dressed as he was in a moderately expensive suit would be pure folly; only fools and drunks, or a combination of both, made targets of themselves by calling attention to the fact that they were well-to-do and likely carrying a wad of greenbacks. In the back alcove he kept hand-me-down clothing for just such situations as this, among the items an old overcoat and a seamen's cap. He stripped off his Chester-field, frock coat, vest, and cravat, and exchanged his hand-tooled shoes for a pair of scuffed boots. With the overcoat buttoned, his trousers and shirt were mostly hidden.

The usual nighttime babel of piano hurdy-gurdy music, the cries of shills and barkers, drunken shouts and laughter, followed Quincannon as he made his way warily along Pacific Street. The Coast had been infamous for nearly half a century as the West's seat of sin and wickedness, a "devil's playground" equaled by none in the country and few in the world. Murders and robber-ies were nightly occurrences, as were every other type of crime and vice. Thieves, cutthroats, footpads, crooked gamblers, pickpockets, bunco steerers, and roaming bands of prostitutes prowled its refuse-littered streets; so did mental defectives, some dangerous, some benign such as "Dirty Tom" McAlear who would eat anything handed him along with a nickel; and so did sports, gay blades, sailors, adventurous citizens of all classes, and addicts on their way to and from the numerous opium dens, many of whom became the predators' victims. So great was the dan-ger that lurked on every street, down every alley, inside every building, that even policemen, armed with pistols and foot-long truncheons, ventured there only in twos and threes after nightfall.

The Red Rooster was just off Stockton, its entrance set back beneath a rococo gallery decorated with plaster images of wisp-ily clad nymphs. More nymphs in various come-hither poses were painted on the outer walls flanking the door. A gaudily dressed barker stood in front, hawking the dubious pleasures to be found within—exotic dancers, games of chance, and "the Coast's most comely and accommodating hostesses." Quincannon stepped around him, then past a burly Kanaka doorman who likely doubled as a bouncer, and stepped inside.

The place was as dimly lighted as Owney had claimed, and so thick with swirling layers of tobacco smoke that the ceiling was nearly invisible. At opposite ends of a long stage at the rear, a pair of honky-tonk pianos were being raucously and tinnily played; in the middle, half a dozen scantily clad dancers were performing a borderline obscene version of the buck-and-wing to whoops of encouragement from the customers. Raised voices and bursts of drunken laughter added to the din.

All of the close-packed tables were occupied, and there was a two-deep cluster at a long bar presided over by a trio of bartenders who, like the doorman, would do double duty when the inevitable brawl broke out. What passed for a dance floor in front of the stage was occupied by men paying a price to publically fondle their female companions. Beyond an open archway, more suckers were busily losing their money in crooked games of roulette, faro, chuck-a-luck, and poker.

Several "hostesses" as scantily clad as the dancers circulated among the throng, some carrying drinks, others engaged in tableside and barside negotiations. None of them were what Quincannon would have described as comely but all were unquestionably accommodating. One buxom blonde had already reached an agreement with an eager customer, the two of them on their way up a rickety-looking sidewall staircase to the rooms upstairs.

Quincannon weaved his way through the main room as if he were searching for a place to sit. There was no point in looking for the men who answered Dinger's and Paddy's descriptions; even if they were present, the poor lighting and crush of bodies made identification impossible unless viewed at close quarters. Instead his sharp eye roamed over the serving and sitting hostesses. It took him some minutes to spy the one he sought, "hefty, with ringlets red as a rooster's comb."

She was seated at a table not far from the stage with three young sailors, all of whom were boiled-owl drunk. One was using his bent arm for a pillow, already passed out; the other two were bickering vigorously over which would be the first to pay for the privilege of sampling Mollie's favors. She wore a bright green, low-cut dress so tight that she bulged in the wrong as well as the right places, and a professional smile as bored as it was pasted on.

Quincannon stepped up beside her chair. The two sailors were so involved in their argument that they failed to notice him lean down close and say, "Hello, Mollie."

Her head lifted and she squinted up at him through the smoke haze. Evidently she liked what she saw; her smile and her voice were no longer bored when she said, "Well, hello, handsome. Don't know you, do I?"

He jerked his head in the direction of the staircase. "You're about to," he said.

Her laugh was as counterfeit as her smile. She said, "I like a gent don't beat around the bush," and got to her feet, taking hold of his arm as soon as she was upright. "And a sober one's all the better."

As they started away, one of the sailors called out a slurred protest that Mollie paid no attention to. At the foot of the stairs she stopped, leaned against Quincannon—assaulting his nostrils with an unholy mix of sour whiskey breath and cheap perfume—and half shouted into his ear, "Two dollars, honey. In advance."

"Two dollars?"

She gave him a lewd wink. "For a good time you'll never forget."

Bah. She must have thought him gullible as well as eager; the going rate in pestholes like the Red Rooster was one dollar. Quincannon had no intention of paying her two dollars, or one dollar, or even the dimes he had bestowed upon Owney. Much less of going upstairs with her.

He thrust her away at arm's length and said in a roughened voice, "I'm not here for a good time, I'm looking for Dinger."

The professional smile vanished. So did the whore's coquettishness; her round face turned visibly hard and wary beneath its thick coating of powder and rouge. "Who?"

"No games, Mollie, and no lies. I know he fancies you and he was here with you Saturday night."

"Yeah? Who told you that?"

"Never mind who. Has he been in tonight?"

"No. He only comes Saturdays. What you want with him?"

"I've got a job for him."

"What kind of job?"

"That's my business and his. Where can I find him?"

"How should I know? I ain't his keeper."

"You know where he hangs his hat?"

"No idea. I ain't never seen him anywhere but here."

"What are his other haunts?"

"No idea."

"Dinger his real name or a moniker?"

"You oughta know; you're lookin' for him."

"Dinger's all I was told. Well?"

"You think he'd give me his right name? Hah!"

"What about his pal, Paddy?"

"Who?"

"The lad he was with Saturday night."

"Oh, him. I don't know him, never seen him before or since."

Both piano players temporarily ceased their dissonant assault, lessening the clamor enough so that when Quincannon spoke again, it was in a voice a few decibels lower. "Listen," he said through a menacing glower, "it's important I see Dinger as soon as possible. This job I got is big and it won't wait. He won't like it if he misses out. *You* won't like it when I tell him you're the reason."

The threat set Mollie to gnawing at her pendulous lower lip. "I swear to you, mister, I dunno where you can find him. But maybe . . . well, maybe there's somebody that does."

"Who would that be?"

"Funderburke."

The name meant nothing to Quincannon and he said so.

"He's one of them does up men's suits," Mollie said.

"You mean a tailor?"

"That's it. Couple of weeks ago Dinger come in wearing a new suit. Black, no stripes, nothin' like the cheap butternuts he favors. Bought it on account of he's in on a sweet business deal, he says, and tips me big that night to prove it. Later on, upstairs, while he was sleepin', I had me a look at the coat, just out of curiosity. That name, Funderburke, was sewn inside the collar."

Simple curiosity had had nothing to do with her examination of the coat, Quincannon thought sardonically. She'd been rummaging in the pockets for Dinger's purse and any stray coins or greenbacks she could safely filch. "Was there an address to go with the name?"

"Not that I seen. Only reason I remember Funderburke is on account of it's such a funny name. That's all I can tell you, mister."

Outside the Red Rooster, Quincannon paused to rid his lungs of tobacco smoke and Mollie's cheap perfume. Funderburke. A slim lead at best. Even if Mollie had remembered the name correctly, her idea of a new suit of quality manufacture was suspect; chances were the tailor was one of the cheapjack variety who sold off-the-rack men's suits and wouldn't know Dinger from hundreds of other walk-in customers. The same was true if Dinger had had enough money to patronize a more respectable tailor. Attempting to track down Funderburke would likely be a waste of time.

Still, it had to be done. His only other options were to give Dinger's name to his contacts in the hope that one of them could turn up an address, or canvass the Coast himself with the same objective—both chancy propositions made even chancier by the possibility that word would reach Dinger of a detective on his trail. Were that to happen, it was liable to spook the coney gang, send them undercover or, worse, away from the Bay Area to set up their operation elsewhere.

Quincannon made his way cautiously out of the heart of the

Coast and down to Kearney Street. A number of the cheapjack tailors did business there, a few of those staying open late to take advantage of the crowds taking part in the nightly Cocktail Route ritual. He found four open and three closed clothing shops sprinkled among the saloons, shooting galleries, painless dentists, astrologists, phrenologists, hypnotists, fortune-tellers such as Madame Louella, and other such businesses of dubious repute. None bore the name Funderburke or any other resembling it.

He debated returning to the agency to reclaim his Chesterfield and check the city business directory. But it was growing late by then, and he was tired—and hungry, having given away his supper to Owney the snitch. The Funderburke search could wait until morning. He went back to Hoolihan's instead, exchanged a second round of insults with Ben Joyce, and partook of the free lunch before riding a cable car home to his flat.

20

QUINCANNON

The city directory provided a listing for a tailor named Funderburke, but the address was something of a surprise. His shop was
on Sutter Street, downtown, which meant that he was at least
moderately successful and catered to a much better class of customer than mugs from the Barbary Coast. Why would Dinger go
to him for a new suit, if in fact he had, when one that would cost
considerably less was available elsewhere? A whim? A flaunting
of newfound wealth? Quincannon set off to find out.

The tailor's shop occupied a modest amount of space on a
block west of Union Square. The plate-glass front window bore
a sign that read: S. FUNDERBURKE, CLOTHING FOR THE DISCERN-
ING GENTLEMAN. The usual bell above the door, more melodious
than most, announced Quincannon's entrance. He had just
enough time to glance around at a small, tasteful display of men's
day and evening apparel and accessories, and to note that there

were no racks of ready-to-wear suits for sale, before a curtain behind a half-counter at the rear parted and a man carrying a measuring tape appeared.

They appraised each other. What Quincannon saw was a large, imposing fellow of some fifty summers, stylishly dressed, with a leonine mane of sandy brown hair and enormous flowing mustaches curled up at the ends. What the other saw was an equally well dressed and evidently well financed potential customer. The welcoming smile he bestowed on Quincannon revealed two sparkling gold teeth.

"Ah, good morning, sir, good morning," he said in a booming voice. "Samuel Funderburke, at your service."

"Good morning. I'm—"

"I can tell that you're a gentleman of discerning taste. A fine suit you're wearing, sir, but Funderburke makes finer, the ultimate, the pinnacle. Perfectly fitted, perfectly tailored from the highest quality cloth."

"No, I—"

"Lamb's wool? Sable-brushed cotton? Tweed for the winter months? Or perhaps it's evening dress that you seek, an elegant tuxedo or tailcoat suit. You'll find no finer craftsmanship anywhere in the city."

"I have no doubt of it, but a new suit isn't the reason I'm here—"

"Casual trousers? Putnam vest? Silk puff tie? Funderburke can supply those as well."

"I'm afraid not. I'm looking for a customer of yours—"

"Not interested in the finest men's wear in San Francisco, sir?

Allow me to show you some samples of my work, and I guarantee you'll change your mind."

"—a man for whom you tailored a suit two weeks ago."

"Ah, then surely he recommended me. A Funderburke customer is a satisfied customer."

Quincannon managed to keep a leash on his patience. "I don't know the man personally. I'm trying to locate him."

"Locate him? Why? For what reason?"

"An important business matter."

"All business matters are important," Funderburke said. "The gentleman's name?"

"He's called Dinger."

"Dinger!" The name had a galvanizing effect on the tailor. His eyes popped wide, his mustaches bristled, he seemed to swell up like a toad. "That louse! That crook! That scum of the earth!"

Quincannon said dryly, "You know him, then."

"Know him? He should show his face here again, Funderburke will strangle him with this measuring tape!"

"What did he do, stiff you for your fee?"

"Stiff me? No one stiffs Funderburke, never! But that louse, that crook, that scum of the earth tried, oh, he tried. Payment with counterfeit money! The gall, the mendacity!"

Ah. It seemed the lead had panned out after all. "A counterfeit hundred-dollar note, mayhap?"

"How did you know? Did that louse, that crook try the same trick on you? Is that why you're looking for him?"

"You could say that. Do you know where I can find him?"

"In jail, if Funderburke had his way."

"But he's not in jail . . . yet."

"I don't know where he is. Where do louses live? Funderburke has no idea."

Quincannon asked, "Did you identify the counterfeit hundred immediately for what it was?"

"A shame and a pity that I didn't, no. It was the teller at my bank." Funderburke's mustaches bristled again. "Seventy dollars in genuine American money I gave that crook in change!"

"But you said no one has ever stiffed you."

"No one has. Funderburke soon got his seventy dollars back, plus thirty for the suit!"

"How, if you don't know where to find Dinger?"

"From his mother."

Quincannon blinked. "His mother?"

"A decent widow lady, not scum like her offspring. I told her I'd have him arrested and sent to prison if he didn't pay me in genuine American currency, and she procured it from him and I from her. A mistake, he told her, he didn't know the bill was counterfeit. Tommyrot!"

"How do you know his mother?"

"The woman who manages my apartment building happens to be a friend of hers. She recommended Funderburke to Esther Jones, Mrs. Jones recommended Funderburke to her louse of a son—more's the pity."

So that was why Dinger had come here for his new suit. "Dinger's last name is Jones, then?"

"Walter Jones." Funderburke barked a humorless laugh. "Dinger! Phooey! Only a crook would have such a stupid nickname!"

"Where does Mrs. Jones reside?"

"On Clay Street. But it won't pay you to talk to her. She wouldn't tell Funderburke where he is, she won't tell you, a stranger."

"I don't suppose your building manager would have any idea of where I can find him."

"If she did, she would have told me."

"I'd like to speak to her, if you have no objection."

Funderburke's eyes slitted briefly, then popped open again. "What do you plan to do to that crook if you find him? Beat him within an inch of his life?"

"Have him arrested."

"Good enough. Talk to Vera Malone, then. Twelve-ninety Powell Street. Talk to his mother. Seventeen-ten Clay. You won't learn anything from them, but I can see you're a persistent gentleman, the same as Funderburke. You'll keep looking until you find that louse, eh?"

"Yes, I will."

"Come back and tell me when you do," the tailor said, "and Funderburke will reward you with a ten percent discount on one of his fine new suits."

Quincannon swung off the Powell Street cable car half a block from number 1290. The three-story residential building sported an ornate façade and an awning-covered entryway, and housed half a dozen flats—a fact confirmed by the row of mailboxes in the foyer. Cards inserted in slots above the boxes identified the tenants. S. Funderburke was one, V. Malone, Mgr., another, so the tailor's word was true.

The building had been fitted with an intercommunication security system that required the pressing of a button in order to gain admittance. Quincannon thumbed the one for V. Malone. Several seconds passed before the buzzer sounded to unlock the entrance door.

The manager's flat was on the first floor, right. A woman was standing in its open doorway when Quincannon entered the inner foyer; he turned in her direction, removing his hat on the way. Middle-aged, plump, and evidently uncorseted, she had graying hair pulled into a bun and a pleasant face marred by a thin growth of black whiskers on her upper lip.

"Mrs. Malone?"

"Miss Malone, if you please."

"Excuse me. My name is Quincannon. I've just come from Samuel Funderburke's tailor shop. He was good enough to let me have his address and your name."

"Was he now. Why? He knows we have no vacancies."

"It isn't a flat I'm seeking, Miss Malone. It's your friend Esther Jones's son, Walter."

The woman eyed him speculatively. "Policeman, are you?"

"No."

"Then why are you looking for him? You don't look like one of his sort."

"A private matter."

"Not the same kind of trouble as Mr. Funderburke had with him?"

"Well . . . yes, I'm afraid so."

"Confound that young whelp! He swore to his mother that he didn't know the bill was counterfeit. She believed him, but I had my doubts. He's shiftless as they come, never possessed so much as a ten-dollar gold piece in his life, at least not one come by honest and sober. And now I find out that counterfeit hundred-dollar note wasn't the only one he had. How many did he give you?"

"I'd rather not say."

"More than just one, then," Miss Malone said, misinterpreting his comment. "The devil only knows where he gets them."

"Have you any idea where he is?"

"No. Esther knows, but she wouldn't tell me. Loyal to a fault, she is. She worships that bibulous rascal—" Miss Malone broke off as a thought struck her. "Now I wonder," she said, more to herself than to Quincannon. "Could those counterfeits have something to do with that trunk?"

"Trunk?"

"No, I suppose not. Wasn't anything valuable in it, so he told Esther. Just old books and things."

"Dinger received a trunk from someone?"

"No, Esther did. Unexpectedly. Walter . . . I refuse to call him by his nickname . . . Walter was living with her at the time and he picked it up at the express office and opened it while she was out on an errand."

"When did the trunk arrive, exactly?"

"Three months ago, about."

"Who sent it, and from where?"

Miss Malone scratched at the hairs on her upper lip. "What difference does it make from where?"

"It may be important."

"I don't see how. Wouldn't have been counterfeit money in a

trunk full of old books and such. I don't know why I thought there might've been. It was sent to Esther, like I said, not Walter."

"I would appreciate knowing its origin just the same."

"Well, I'd rather not say," Miss Malone said staunchly. "It's Esther's private business, poor woman. I shouldn't have mentioned the trunk in the first place."

Quincannon gave it up. Prodding her any further would only put her back up. He shifted topics instead, asking, "Is the name Paddy Lasher familiar to you?"

"Lasher? No, I can't say it is. Who is he, one of Walter's good-for-nothing comrades?"

"You might say that. A heavyset man with a thick mustache and one brown and one blue eye. Have you ever seen Walter with anyone who answers that description?"

"No, and I hope I never do. Is this man Lasher involved with the counterfeit money?"

"Perhaps."

"If you find Walter, I suppose you'll have him arrested. It will break poor Esther's heart if he's put in prison."

"I may not have any choice in the matter."

Miss Malone sighed. "You know, there was a time when I wished I'd married and had children of my own, but watching Walter grow up put that notion right out of my head."

There was nothing more to be learned from Vera Malone. Quincannon thanked her and exited the building just in time to swing onto a cable car headed back downtown.

21

SABINA

She was thinking of silencing the rumblings in her stomach with a meal at the tearoom around the corner when John came bounding in. Just in time, or so she thought at first. The prospect of having more filling fare in his company in Pop Hoffman's Café or another good restaurant brightened her welcoming smile. But food was not what was on his mind.

"Ah, you're still here," he said as he closed the door. "I was afraid you might have gone out."

"I was just about to. Now you can join me for luncheon—"

"No time for a leisurely meal today, my dear. I need you to do me a favor this afternoon if you have no plans."

"What sort of favor?"

"Interview a woman whose son has been passing those counterfeit hundred-dollar bills."

"Oh, so you've uncovered a firm lead. I thought you might be on the trail when you came and went so swiftly earlier."

"A lead, yes, thanks to a stroke of luck. But a stalled one at the moment." He went on to explain about the information given him by Barbary Coast scruff Owney, the Red Rooster prostitute Mollie, the tailor Funderburke, and Esther Jones's friend Vera Malone.

Sabina said dubiously, "And you think I may be able to convince Dinger's mother to reveal his whereabouts, is that it?"

"You stand a better chance than I do. A woman is apt to confide more readily in a member of her own sex."

"Not in this case. I'm as much of a stranger to her as you are. Chances are she wouldn't even talk to me."

"She might, with the proper approach."

"Meaning the use of feminine wiles."

"Of which you're blessed with a considerable amount."

"Oh, bosh. Frankly, I don't much like the idea of resorting to trickery to deceive a protective mother."

"The son she's protecting is a criminal helping to take honest citizens for a ride. Mrs. Jones's loyalty is misplaced."

"Perhaps so, but no matter how I approached her or what I said, it's quite unlikely that I could induce her to betray him. And you know it."

"I have great faith in your abilities, my dear, as I hope I made clear on Saturday evening."

"Soft soap has no effect on me, John. You ought to know that, too, by now."

"Even if you're unable to pry loose Dinger's whereabouts, you may have success in finding out from whence came the trunk Vera Malone mentioned. That knowledge could prove to be important."

"What are you thinking it contained besides old books?" Sabina asked skeptically. "Counterfeit bills made by Long Nick Darrow?"

"Not many, if so. The ones currently being passed were manufactured by a photoengraving process not in use ten years ago."

"What, then?"

"I don't know," John admitted. "Perhaps I'm grasping at straws, but I have a hunch Dinger's involvement in the new coney game is somehow connected to that trunk."

A hunch, she thought wryly—the male equivalent of feminine intuition, which he had been known to scoff at.

"If I'm wrong," he went on, "then that avenue of investigation can be eliminated. But I won't know if I am or not until I know who sent the trunk and for what reason."

It seemed to Sabina that the wisest course of action was to turn over to Mr. Boggs what he'd discovered about Dinger and Paddy Lasher. But John was mulish when he was on the trail of lawbreakers, and inclined as always to chase personal glory as well as the causes of justice. Not that he had any intention of attempting to prove his methods superior to those of the Secret Service and his former chief. It was ingrained in his nature to act as he did, right or wrong, and she had long ago given up trying to change him. But on the other hand, she didn't have to aid and abet him, did she?

He smiled at her and said in gently cajoling tones, "So will you please make an effort to see Esther Jones and find out whatever you can?"

She sighed. The answer to the question she'd just asked herself was yes, she did, at least in this instance. "Very well," she said. "But it will cost you."

"Cost me?"

"Dinner at a restaurant of my choosing. Delmonico's, perhaps."

John winced—Delmonico's was among the city's most exclusive dining emporiums—but he knew better than to argue. "Anywhere you like, my dear. Your wish is my command."

The gallantry was a trifle forced, but she appreciated it nonetheless.

Seventeen-ten Clay Street was a large two-story structure, once a private residence, now a middle-to-low-income boardinghouse. It was the sort of neighborhood Sabina had expected from the address, and justified her decision to remove the jeweled barrette from her upswept hair, her seed-pearl earrings, and her Charles Horner hatpin, and to don a less stylish cape, before leaving the agency. The decision was further justified by a ROOM TO LET sign on the front gate: it gave her just the right opening gambit for the ruse she intended to employ. Now if Mrs. Esther Jones was home and in a receptive mood . . .

She was. Sabina found her sweeping the floor in the front hallway, a thin middle-aged woman with sad eyes, careworn hands, and a lined and wrinkled face. A woman who had known considerable sorrow in what had not been an easy life, she judged.

"I'm Mrs. Jones, the landlady. What can I do for you, miss?"

"I saw your sign," Sabina said, smiling. "How large is the room being let?"

"Good-sized. Second-floor rear, overlooks a bit of a garden. Nice and airy."

"And how much are you asking?"

"Twenty-five dollars a month."

"Mmm. I'm not sure I can afford that much just now . . ."

"Breakfast included."

"Well . . . may I see it?"

"Take you right up."

Sabina followed Mrs. Jones up the uncarpeted stairs, down a bisecting hallway to a door bearing the numeral 3. The room was more or less as the woman had described it, functionally and somewhat skimpily furnished, spotlessly clean. Esther Jones was a punctilious housekeeper.

Time for the ruse. Sabina felt a pang of regret at the need for deception—she disliked lying, especially to honest, hardworking individuals who had already suffered hardships—but if the woman's son was involved with the counterfeiting ring as John believed, it was in a just cause.

"It's a nice room," she said. "That wall there would be perfect for my books. That is, if you have no objection to bookcases being brought in."

"Well . . . how many bookcases?"

"Two or three, depending on the exact measurements."

"You must have a lot of books, miss."

"Yes, I do. I'm employed in a secondhand bookshop downtown, you see, and my employer lets me have unsold volumes either free or at nominal prices. Nothing rare or valuable, of course."

"He must be a good man to work for."

"He is. Have you many books yourself, Mrs. Jones?"

The woman shook her head. "I'm not much of a reader."

"The reason I asked," Sabina said, "is that my employer is always in the market for new acquisitions. I thought that perhaps you might have some for sale." She feigned a self-deprecating smile. "I sometimes act as a scout for him, for a small stipend to supplement my salary."

Mrs. Jones brushed at a loose strand of graying hair. "What kind of books is he interested in?"

"Oh, all kinds, especially rare volumes and sets. Do you have any you'd be willing to sell?"

"Well . . . a trunkful my sister had come to me a while back."

"Really? I wish I had a relative who was that thoughtful."

"Wasn't a matter of being thoughtful. She died three months ago."

"Oh. I'm sorry to hear that."

"Well, she was in poor health for some time. A widow like me, didn't have much. Put in her will that I was to have the family mementos she'd stored up, photographs and such and our pa's old books."

"Did she live in this area?"

"No. Up north."

"The Pacific Northwest, by any chance? I have a relative in Seattle."

"That so? Seattle's where Maureen lived."

"Small world," Sabina said through her fixed smile. "May I ask what business her husband was in?"

Wrong question, too personal. Esther Jones's face closed up.

"I'm sorry, I didn't mean to pry," Sabina said. "I guess I'm just a nosey parker."

One thin shoulder lifted, dropped. "No offense. You want to look at the books? I doubt they're worth much."

"They may be, one can never tell."

"They're down in the basement."

A flight of stairs led from the ground floor into a musty, gaslit basement dominated by an old coal-burning furnace. At one end was a wire-fenced storage area—four separate units with padlocked doors, one each for Mrs. Jones and her tenants. The largest of them, which she proceeded to unlock, contained a jumble of items, one of which was an old, battered, brassbound trunk set atop a rickety table.

"Books're in there," Mrs. Jones said. "Didn't see any reason for my son to take 'em out."

"Oh, your son lives here with you?"

A tic fluttered the woman's left eye. "No, he don't. Not anymore."

Sabina said brightly, "I hope he didn't move too far away."

"Why would you hope that?"

"Why, for your sake, Mrs. Jones. Mothers always like to have their children close by. Mine certainly did."

"He's got his own life to live," the woman said with more than a trace of bitterness. "Go on in, miss. Trunk's not locked."

The subject of the son was now closed as well; any more questions would only arouse suspicion. Sabina stepped inside and bent to the trunk.

A large label on its top confirmed that it had been shipped from Seattle. It provided the name and address of the drayage firm, and was stamped with the date of shipment, slightly more than three months ago. She committed the information to memory as she lifted the trunk's lid.

The books were in a haphazard jumble, as if they had been taken out and then tossed back by the handful. Dinger Jones's doing. No reputable drayage firm would pack in such a careless fashion. Sabina removed them a few at a time, some threescore in total. There was nothing else in the trunk.

"Worth anything?" Mrs. Jones asked.

Sabina was hardly an expert, but she knew books well enough to judge that this lot was composed entirely of inexpensive editions of populist fiction and nonfiction. Her feelings about this were mixed. The books' relative worthlessness made it unnecessary to keep up the pretense of interest in them and relieved her of any further responsibility, but she also felt sorry that Esther Jones would receive no money for them. If they had had value, she would have felt obligated to notify a reputable secondhand book dealer on the woman's behalf.

She said truthfully, "I'm afraid not."

"Figured as much. Walter said they were just junk."

"Walter?"

The question earned Sabina nothing but a headshake.

She returned the books to the trunk, stacking them neatly. When she was finished, Mrs. Jones relocked the wire door and led the way upstairs. In the foyer she said, "About the room, miss. Yours if you want it."

"I do like it, but . . . I have to make sure I can afford the rent before I decide."

"Don't take too long. There's other interest."

Which, if true, was a salve on Sabina's conscience. She said, "Thank you for showing it to me, Mrs. Jones, and for allowing me to look through your books. I really am sorry they're not valuable."

"Don't be. I didn't expect any different."

When Sabina stepped off the trolley on Market Street, she went straight to Western Union where she composed a wire to the Pinkerton office in Seattle. She included the information she'd gleaned from the trunk label, and requested that at the expense of Carpenter and Quincannon, Professional Detective Services, an operative be directed to trace the shipper and determine the name of Esther Jones's deceased sister. She also requested background data on the sister and her family, in particular any known or suspected criminal activity.

John was at his desk when she entered the agency. What she'd learned from Mrs. Jones satisfied him, though he would have been more pleased if she had managed to uncover a lead to Dinger's whereabouts. Fortunately for him, he didn't say so. He praised the cleverness of her book ruse, but he was less enthusiastic when she told him of her request to the Seattle Pinkerton office.

"An operative on the task full-time will cost us dearly," he said, "and with no chance of reimbursement from the government."

"We can afford it. And it was the only way to find out what you need to know. Of course, I can wire a cancellation if you'd rather turn the matter over to Mr. Boggs."

"No, no. I don't want to burden him with what may turn out to be a false lead."

"But you don't think it will be. Nor do I. The fact that Seattle was the trunk's origin indicates it contained more than just old books and family mementos."

He admitted that it was likely. His stubborn determination to be the one to track down Dinger Jones and Paddy Lasher remained undaunted. Like a bloodhound on the scent, he refused to give up the chase until his quarry was tracked down— an admirable quality in a detective when it wasn't carried to extremes.

"Was Long Nick Darrow married?" Sabina asked.

"No. At least, not that I was able to determine during my investigation. Were you thinking that Esther Jones's sister was Darrow's widow?"

"The possibility occurred to me. Assuming, of course, that Darrow did in fact die that night ten years ago."

"Even if he didn't, what possible connection could he have had with the married sister?"

"An illicit affair?"

"Unlikely," John said. "He was a loner as well as a villainous cuss, and evidently confined his interest in women to prostitutes. I find it hard to believe he would have entrusted anything to any woman, much less material related to his coney racket."

"If the sister did have such material in her possession, she may not have known she had it."

"Hidden in her belongings without her knowledge? Possibly. But not by Darrow, I'll warrant."

"A confederate of his, then? He did have confederates?"

"Yes, several. All now either dead or in prison."

"One could have filched some of the counterfeit bills," Sabina pointed out, "and a cache of them what Dinger found."

"True enough, but as I told you earlier, the queer being passed now is not the same as the ones manufactured by Darrow's gang."

"Could the new bogus notes have been made using his old ones as a prototype?"

"It's possible to copy Darrow's method of bill-splitting," John said, "but in order to produce such certificates as the one Mr. Boggs showed me, a new set of plates would be needed."

"Could duplicates be made from the plates Darrow used?"

"Yes, if the engraver was skilled enough. But as I also told you, those plates were destroyed in the fire."

"Are you absolutely sure of that?"

"The printing press and a stack of counterfeit notes were in plain sight in the warehouse when the other agents and I entered. So was Thomas Cooley, the engraver who made the plates, so they must have been there, too. Darrow wouldn't have let them out of his sight."

"What happened to Cooley?"

"Killed in the raid, by one of the other agents' bullets."

Sabina spread her hands, palms up. "Well, then, what *could* have been tucked away in the trunk that Dinger found and that led to the current counterfeiting operation?"

Rhetorical question. John wagged his head, fluffed his beard.

"The Pinkerton report may provide a clue," she said. "But if it doesn't?"

"Then I'll pry the answer from Dinger. Or Paddy Lasher."

"If you can find them."

"I'll find them," he vowed. "One way or another."

22

QUINCANNON

There was no word from the Seattle Pinkerton office on Wednesday. Nor word from Ezra Bluefield or any of Quincannon's other contacts on the whereabouts of Dinger Jones and Paddy Lasher. But on Thursday morning—

It was Slewfoot who provided the first lead to Lasher, when Quincannon stopped at the vendor's newsstand for a copy of the *Argonaut*. Slewfoot, who had the miraculous ability to see clearly from behind his dark glasses when the need arose, glanced around to make sure no one was in earshot before he said in an undertone, "I've a bit of information for you, Mr. Q., might help you find one of the lads you're looking for."

"Dinger?"

"No, Paddy Lasher. The name of a lad what knows him. Ben Baxter."

"I don't know the name. Who is he?"

"Used to be in the shanghaiing trade, worked with Lasher back then."

"And doing what now?"

"Nothing much. Retired on account of his health, what's left of it. Word is Lasher supplies him with foot juice for old times' sake."

"Foot juice" was cheap red wine, of the sort sold at wine dumps such as Jack Foyle's on Stockton Street. "Where can I find Baxter?"

Slewfoot paused to sell another newspaper. Then, when they were alone again, "Clayton Hotel, Vallejo Street. He lives there, watches over the desk."

"Is it alcohol that ruined his health?"

"That and bad arthritis, so I been told."

The information was worth a silver dollar. Slewfoot, as was his habit, bit into the coin to make sure it was genuine before slipping it into his pocket. No one ever had or was ever likely to pass off a counterfeit coin or bill on the wily news vendor.

Quincannon had been on his way to the agency. Now he reversed direction and climbed Stockton Street to Jack Foyle's, where he paid a nickel for a quart of foot juice drawn from one of the barrels behind the long bar. The Mason jar into which it went was cracked and dirty—the hodgepodge of containers used in Foyle's were all unsanitary—but the warped lid fit well enough to keep any of the foul stuff from slopping out. The bartender provided a paper sack for which he had the audacity to charge an extra penny.

The two-story Clayton Hotel was one of several run-down

hotels and lodging houses beyond Broadway at the edge of the Barbary Coast. Its sign was so small and weather-faded that Quincannon almost walked by without spying it. The odors of dry rot, stale tobacco smoke, stale wine, and even less pleasant substances assailed him when he entered. There was nothing in the tiny lobby except a none-too-stable-looking staircase to the upper floor, and next to it, a cubbyhole desk fronted by a waist-high board partition.

From the doorway, it looked as though no one was inside the cubbyhole. But as Quincannon crossed to it, the warped and un-swept floor creaking underfoot, a grizzled head appeared above the countertop. The man had been slouched down in an ancient morris chair, its stuffing bleeding through several rips and tears in the fabric. Asleep, evidently, for he rubbed at his eyes as he struggled to sit up.

He was a wreck of an individual who might have lived any-where between forty and sixty years. Rheumy, blood-flecked eyes under which purplish pouches hung. Sunken cheeks coated with gray whiskers, greasy hair straggling from under a cracked leather cap, a bulbous nose disfigured by broken blood vessels. His hands, clawlike, the wrist joints and knuckles bulging with ar-thritic knots, trembled slightly when he moved them.

"Ben Baxter?"

The rheumy eyes peered up at Quincannon. "Who wants to know?" he said in a voice as raspy as a file on wood. The words were clear enough, not slurred but quivery. The shakiness and the bloodshot eyes indicated he was suffering from alcohol deprivation.

"A pal of Paddy Lasher."

"Yeah? I know Paddy's pals and you ain't one of 'em."

"I am now. Flynn's the name. He didn't mention me?"

"No. Why should he?"

"We're in the game together."

"What game?"

"He didn't tell you that, either? Just as well. It's not smart to talk about it the way Dinger does, even to pals."

"Who's Dinger?"

"I thought you said you knew all of Paddy's pals."

"I don't know *you*," Baxter said. "What you want with me?"

"I don't want anything from you. Just doing a favor for Paddy."

"What favor?"

"He asked me to bring you this." Quincannon produced the paper sack, set it on the countertop, and removed the jar of foot juice from inside.

Baxter stared at the jar, a tongue more gray than pink flicking out to lick cracked lips. The bloodshot gaze was avid.

"Well, now," he said. "Well, now."

Gambling that Lasher had been kept too busy passing counterfeit bills to pay social visits, Quincannon said, "It's been a while since Paddy's been to see you and he knew I had business up this way today."

Baxter leaned forward, reached up with both deformed hands. His arthritic fingers locked around the jar, pulled it down to him, then he managed to twist the cap off, lift the jar, and drink deeply—all without spilling a drop. He smacked his lips, wiped his mouth with the back of a not very clean hand.

"Good old Paddy. He don't never forget his pals, even if he don't come around much anymore."

"There'll be plenty more where this came from," Quincannon said, "and of better quality, too, now that he's in the chips."

"Wish I could've got into the dodge with him," Baxter said. He drank again. "But these goddamn hands . . . I can't hardly do nothing no more. Hurt like hell day and night. This here medicine's all that helps."

"So he did tell you about the game, eh, Ben? About him and Dinger shoving the queer."

"Never said nothing about nobody named Dinger. Hinted about the game. Always did like to brag when he's into something good, and he knows I ain't one to flap my gums." Baxter added bitterly, "Knows I can't never go out no more on account of the goddamn arthur-itis, neither."

"His hints include how he got into the game? Or who's running it?"

"Nah. And I didn't ask."

"Good. Do you happen to know where he hangs his hat?"

Baxter took another long pull from the jar. "Sure. Ain't you seen him there?"

"No. Only at the place where the queer's being made."

"Where you hang *your* hat, Flynn?"

"Down near the Embarcadero."

"Yeah? Which end?"

"North. The warehouse district."

"Paddy's up that way, too." Baxter drank again. The jar was more than half empty now. As Quincannon had hoped, the foot juice had loosened the old mug's tongue and was making him flap his gums in spite of his claim to the contrary. "Got the waterfront in his blood. Me and him used to be in business together, he tell you that?"

"Mentioned it. The crimping dodge."

"Man, them was the days. Made plenty of scratch, spent it all on liquor and whores." He cackled reminiscently. "Not cheap whores, neither. Young and fancy, all sizes and colors."

"Whereabouts is Paddy's crib?" Quincannon said. "Maybe I'll go look him up there."

"Icehouse Alley."

"What number?"

Baxter frowned and said muzzily, "Can't rightly recollect. Oughtn't to say anyways, even to a pal of his. He wouldn't like it."

"He won't know because I won't tell him. Try to remember the address, Ben, would you?"

Baxter tried, scrunch-faced, but the foot juice had taken its toll on his memory. Finally he shook his head. "Icehouse Alley ain't big," he said, "you'll find him easy enough." He took another swig from the jar, swiped a hand across his mouth, and treated Quincannon to a slobbery grin. "You're a pal, Flynn. You and Paddy, real pals."

Quincannon turned away. Behind him Baxter said, "Come back any time, I'm always here. And bring some more medicine for my goddamn arthur-itis when you do."

Icehouse Alley.

A one-block, dead-end lane close to the Embarcadero, obviously named for a vanished icehouse. This seemed to be his time for dealing with icehouses present and past, Quincannon thought wryly, though there was no evidence of the one that had once operated here. Now the narrow street was lined with nondescript lodging houses, vacant lots, and on the Green Street corner, a saloon called Mulrooney's Rest.

Quincannon ventured along the alley's short length, looking at the dwelling places in passing. There was nothing to be gained by stopping at each one to examine mailboxes; even if Paddy Lasher was using his own name, which was problematic given his evident passion for privacy, it was highly doubtful that he would advertise the location of his lair.

In total there were six lodging houses, ranging in size from two-story structures containing several units to single-story structures of two and three rooms each. It wouldn't take long to canvass them all, but in waterfront neighborhoods such as this, those tenants who were in residence at midday would be wary of strangers knocking on their doors and closemouthed as a result.

He returned to the corner and entered Mulrooney's Rest. Saloons were often the best place to gather information, barmen being more inclined to view a stranger asking casual questions with a less jaundiced eye than the average citizen. This one was a typical workingman's neighborhood tavern, its only distinctive feature a large oil painting suspended on the wall above the bar of a buxom, seminude woman reclining on a couch. The artist was either myopic or poorly versed in anatomical reconstruction; the nude's bulging collarbone made it seem as if she had three breasts.

The dozen or so patrons, most of whom were drinking beer and partaking of the free lunch, gave Quincannon the usual once-over as he bellied up to the long plank anchored atop a row of barrels. The bartender, a thin, fox-faced fellow wearing bright pink sleeve garters, came over to ask, "What'll it be?"

"Beer." Which Quincannon had no intention of drinking.

The bartender drew a pint, set the chipped mug before him. Quincannon said conversationally as he paid his nickel, "I'm told an old acquaintance of mine lives in Icehouse Alley, but not in which house. Mayhap you can tell me, if he's a customer of yours."

"What's his name?"

"He answers to more than one, for good reasons of his own. You'll know him if you ever saw him. Large gent, thick black mustache, one brown eye and one blue."

The description brought a bored headshake. "Can't help you, mister," the barman said, and moved away to answer a customer's call for more beer.

"He can't but I can," a man on Quincannon's left said. He sidled closer, a weathered old salt dressed in a seaman's cap and pea jacket. "Couldn't help overhearing. Different-colored eyes, I never seen the like. Nature sure plays funny tricks sometimes."

"That she does. You know him, then."

"No, but I seen him a few times."

"The name he's using?"

"Never heard it. Keeps to himself. I asked him once about those eyes and he told me to mind my own business."

"You happen to know where he lives?"

"Right next door to where I room. My window looks straight across at his. Mostly he keeps his curtains drawn, but I seen him in there once when they wasn't."

"Which house is he in?"

"Last one at the end, next to the empty lot where the old ice-house used to set."

Quincannon put another nickel on the bar, pushed it and his untouched beer over in front of the old salt. "My thanks."

"And mine to you, laddy." Then, his nose in his glass as Quin-cannon turned away, "One brown, one blue—I never seen the like."

The designated lodging house at the end of Icehouse Alley was a single-story, unpainted frame dwelling that contained a pair of adjoining units. The one on the near side had to be Paddy Lasher's, for its side window faced toward the two-story build-ing next door.

Glances in both directions assured Quincannon that the alley was presently empty of foot and vehicle traffic. Without slowing his pace, he turned up a cracked cement walkway and climbed three steps to the door, his hand inside his coat and rest-ing on the handle of his holstered Navy Colt. If Lasher was home, there would be no shilly-shallying; the pistol would come out immediately. He had enough circumstantial evidence against the mug to place him under citizen's arrest, after which he would hie him off to the Secret Service office at the Mint. Mr. Boggs and his operatives would soon enough pry loose the names and whereabouts of Lasher's partners in the coney game, pos-sessing as they did less violent methods of persuasion than those at Quincannon's disposal.

But there was no answer to his knuckle raps on the door. In-stead of the Navy, then, he drew out his set of lock picks. When he was sure he remained alone and unobserved, he set to work with the picks. The door lock was no match for his expertise; he had the tumblers free in less than a minute. He opened the door just long enough to ease himself through.

Drawn curtains over the side window rendered the room semidark. Outside he had noted wires strung here from a nearby electric light pole; he located the wall switch, turned it. A fly-specked ceiling globe flickered on, steadied, and brought the interior into clear view.

There were two rooms, the one he was in and a smaller one that served as sleeping quarters. Lasher had lived here for some time, evidently, and none too tidily; the rooms were cluttered with furniture, strewn clothing, unwashed dishes.

Quincannon began a systematic search. What he discovered in the bedroom wardrobe and dresser was a disparate array of items that rightly belonged to many individuals other than Paddy Lasher. A brand-new set of surveyor's tools. A brass sextant. Purses, billfolds, and handbags, some expensively made and all empty. A small store of valuable men's and women's rings and bracelets. A gold double hunter pocket watch with chain and engraved fob. A fashionable beaver fur stole. Now he knew how Lasher had supported himself before graduating to federal crime—as a thief and dispenser of stolen goods.

Also in the wardrobe was a new, well-tailored suit of the sort Samuel Funderburke had made for Dinger Jones. Quincannon searched the pockets, found them empty. None of the other hanging garments provided him with any connection to the coney racket. Nor did anything else he examined in both rooms, including the dusty floor under Lasher's unmade bed.

Now what?

Quincannon perched on the edge of a mohair chair to

consider. He could wait here for Lasher's return, but that might take hours, if not considerably longer. There was no food in the apartment, and the meal residue on the unwashed plates was crusted solid; Lasher may well have spent one or more nights elsewhere and intend to do so again tonight. Besides, Quincannon hadn't the patience for an extended vigil in this iniquitous den.

What he should do, then, was to take what he'd learned directly to Mr. Boggs and let the government agents pursue Lasher and Dinger Jones. He'd done an admirable job of uncovering their names and involvement in the coney game, hadn't he? Of course he had, and Mr. Boggs would be properly appreciative. Still, he was reluctant to abandon his own investigation just yet, without some lead to the identity of the man running the operation and where the counterfeit bills were being manufactured.

Even so, it seemed that now, stymied as he was, he had little choice in the matter. He might as well go ahead and unburden himself to Mr. Boggs.

As he started to lift himself from the chair, his eye caught and held on the wardrobe, visible through the open doorway between the rooms. Specifically, the curved pediment once meant to be decorative, now as timeworn as the rest of the piece that it surmounted. He reentered the bedroom, pulled a ladderback chair over in front of the wardrobe, climbed up on it, and felt around behind the pediment.

His first exploration found nothing. But when he moved the chair to the left and tried on the other side, his fingers encountered metal—a metal box stuffed down onto the wardrobe's recessed top. Ah! He had to move the chair again and stretch up and around to get a firm grip on the box, then lift it out of its nest of dust.

It was an old steel strongbox, heavy and locked. The lock was no match for his picks; he had it open in no time. Paddy Lasher's private trove. A man's valuable gold ring set with a fat ruby, likely another piece of robbery loot. A chamois pouch containing four gold double eagles and five eagles. A glass vial of white powdery substance which Quincannon judged to be morphine. Three hundred-dollar banknotes which he could tell by close eye-squint and feel were newly minted counterfeits. And last but by no means least, a small torn piece of butcher paper on which was scrawled in a childish hand: *J 72 Folsom 2.*

Some sort of code?

No, by godfrey. Abbreviations. *J*—an initial. 72 Folsom 2— an address, 72 Folsom Street, unit number 2.

Quincannon relocked the box with his pick, replaced it behind the pediment. As he stepped down off the chair, his mouth quirked into one of his basilisk smiles. He wouldn't have to abandon his investigation yet after all. Not if his guesses were correct and the address belonged to either Dinger Jones or, better yet, the head koniaker whose name might also begin with a *J.*

23

SABINA

The morning having been quiet and uneventful, Sabina took a longer than usual noontime break. On Geary Street just off Market was one of her favorite luncheon places, the Midtown Bakery, which specialized in custard-filled éclairs, scones with clotted cream, and other pastries of the sort favored by Cousin Callie. Unlike Callie, whose sweet tooth had broadened her hips and waistline, Sabina had been blessed with the ability to eat anything she chose, in any quantity, without gaining an ounce; her weight was the same as it had been as a young girl, her figure just as svelte.

The bakery's more sugary confections held no appeal for her today, however. She lunched on two extra-large buttered muffins, one banana and one blueberry, a glass of milk, and a cup of tea. And bought a chocolate chip cookie to take back to the agency for a mid-afternoon snack.

The afternoon mail had arrived in her absence, and along with it, a messenger-delivered Western Union telegram. At her desk she glanced through the mail, none of which was important enough to be opened immediately, and then turned her attention to the wire. Intuition told her that it was from the Seattle Pinkerton office. If so, John should be the one to read it first. But she couldn't *know* who it was from without opening it, and she, after all, had been the one to send the original request. She picked up her letter opener, slit the envelope, and removed the wire.

Yes, it was from the Pinks office in Seattle. A rather lengthy synopsis of their findings, semicoded as usual in sensitive cases and ending with the phrase "full report to follow by mail." And an enlightening conspectus it was.

The shipping firm whose name and address were on the trunk label had been hired by a law firm in charge of the estate of Maureen Cooley, deceased sister of Esther Jones. Mrs. Cooley had been a childless widow of little means. Her husband, Thomas Cooley, a printer and engraver by trade, had served four years in the Washington State penitentiary on a forgery charge. And his involvement in the counterfeiting of United States currency had led to his death, as John had told her, during the April 1887 warehouse raid.

The answer to what Dinger Jones had found in the trunk seemed clear to Sabina now. The plates made by Thomas Cooley had not been destroyed in the fire; John was wrong about that. For some reason, Cooley must have liberated the plates shortly before the incursion. There were at least two possible explanations: Darrow had gotten wind that government agents were close on his trail and made plans to move his counterfeiting operation elsewhere; or Cooley had had a falling-out with Darrow, and decided to skip out with the plates and establish a new coney game of his own. That part of the truth might never be known.

In any event, Cooley must have taken the plates home and hidden them in the trunk containing his wife's family possessions. He hadn't informed her of the fact, and when both he and Darrow were killed—there seemed little doubt now that Long Nick had failed to survive his plunge into the harbor—the plates had languished undiscovered for a decade. And representatives of the law firm had not seen fit to take inventory of the trunk's contents before arranging for shipment to Esther Jones.

What had her son done after finding them? Taken the plates to Paddy Lasher, who had in turn passed them on to a local printer/engraver who then used them as prototypes for the new, photoengraved plates? Or had Dinger himself known of such an individual? In any event, it seemed probable that that unknown, whoever he might be, was "boss" of the present operation.

The proper procedure, even more so now with this information, was to turn the investigation over to Mr. Boggs and his operatives; it was their job to round up Lasher and Jones, identify the ringleader and the place where the bogus notes were being manufactured. But would John agree, or stubbornly insist on continuing to pursue his own course of action? Briefly, very briefly, Sabina considered contacting Mr. Boggs herself. But that would be a breach of their partnership trust and John might never forgive her. No, she would have to rely on her powers of persuasion, if not his good judgment.

And where was John? He had not presented himself at the office this morning, as he had told her last night he intended to do, nor did it seem that he'd put in an appearance during her noon-hour absence. Off somewhere chasing a lead that had come his way or on one of his hunches. He could be irresponsibly secretive when he was on the scent. And too often inclined to rush in where fools feared to tread . . .

Oh, stop acting like a mother hen, she told herself. *What happened to Stephen is not going to happen to John. He has survived twentysome years of adventures far more dangerous than the present undertaking, and he'll go right on surviving. Why must you worry so about him? You didn't for most of the previous six years of the relationship.*

I didn't love him then. Now I do.

The self-admission was not a little jarring. She had carefully avoided the word "love" in her thoughts about John; never quite been willing to admit that her feelings for him had deepened to an emotional level akin to that she'd had for Stephen. Stephen was the only man to whom she'd said, "I love you," out loud or to herself. But now . . .

There was no denying it any longer. She was in love with John Frederick Quincannon, despite or perhaps in part because of his shortcomings and his less than endearing traits.

24

QUINCANNON

72 Folsom 2 turned out to be a surprise.

An address, yes, but not a lodging house, hotel, or other type of residence as he'd expected.

A harness and saddlery shop, or rather what was left of one.

Part of one half of the old building had been charred by a fire that had spread to and damaged its roof, as well as the side wall of an ironworks firm next door. The fire hadn't been recent; there was no odor of burned wood, and the plywood square nailed across what had presumably been a side window had a weather-warped appearance. A handmade sign on the locked front entrance read: CLOSED UNTIL FURTHER NOTICE. T. HOOPER, PROP.

A narrow areaway separated the harness shop from its fire-scorched neighbor, but it was impassably choked with blackened debris. There was no such passage on the opposite side, merely a tall board fence separating it from the business next door. The lot was deep—deep enough so that a second structure existed behind the shop? That might well be the meaning of the numeral 2 in the scrawled street address.

Quincannon half circled the block. A carriageway bisected it, giving access to the buildings that fronted on Folsom and Howard. The harness shop had been fifth from the corner; when he reached that point in the presently empty carriageway, he could see the backside of an outbuilding above another tall board fence.

The fence had no access door. He jumped to catch hold of its top, lifted himself up, held there long enough to determine that the outbuilding was squat and gray-shingled—a storage shed, likely—and that there was enough room to pass between its near wall and the boundary fence, and then swung over and down.

He made his way around to the front of the shed. Its wide single door was secured by a heavy brass padlock, the staples hooked through an iron hasp. He tested the padlock, squinting at the keyhole. Stout, fairly new, and of quality manufacture. He ought to be able to pick it, but doing so would take time. There might be an easier way of gaining entrance—a window in the side wall he had just passed by.

He went back to it. Locked, but neither shuttered nor barred. He cleared off a section of outside grime with his palm, laid an eye close to the glass. The inside of the pane was also dirty and flyspecked, but he could make out enough of the interior to identify the various shapes that crowded it.

Much of the contents appeared to be business storage: saddles and saddlemaker's forms; various types of harness hung on wall hooks; a stack of leather skins; buckles, rings, and other hardware on a bench beneath the window. But there was also a cot covered by a heavy blanket, a table with a lantern on it, a small oil stove, what appeared to be an old steamer trunk. Crude living quarters. Dinger's, no doubt. Not as a squatter, but with the permission of T. Hooper.

Was Hooper the ringleader? Unlikely, given his profession. Probably an old acquaintance of Dinger's talked into providing temporary lodgings. Was Jones still occupying the premises, or had he made enough from passing queer to have moved to more agreeable accommodations? A good look around inside might provide the answer.

The window's sash had been tightly latched into its frame, but not so tightly as to avoid a small amount of play when Quincannon pushed upward. He took out his pocket knife, opened and slid the largest blade into the crack at the bottom, and tried maneuvering it inside to get at the latch. But the opening was too narrow, the sash too well embedded. Blast! The only way he could enter through the window was to break the glass, and he was not about to do that. He would have to try picking the padlock—

Sounds, shuffling footsteps.

He was no longer alone on the property.

He stood motionless, ears straining. Whoever it was crossed the weedy patch of open space between the shop and the shed, the single set of steps neither slow nor rapid. The rattling and scraping sounds that followed could only be the opening of the padlock. Then came the creaking of wood as the door was opened, then closed again seconds later.

Quincannon crouched for another squint through the window glass. The man inside was an indistinct shape until a match flared and the table lantern bloomed with light. Medium height, red face, crooked nose that had once been broken and improperly set, and when he removed his hat and tossed it onto the cot, a head speckled-egg bald, a face as red as Mollie's hair and a rooster's comb.

Dinger Jones had returned to his lair.

Jones wore a plain sack coat, striped trousers, and scuffed half boots, all of which he immediately began to remove. Down to a pair of baggy long johns, he helped himself to a swig from a pint of whiskey perched on the table next to the lantern. Then he opened the steamer trunk, rummaged around inside, and produced what appeared to be the coat and trousers of his new S. Funderburke-tailored suit.

Quincannon ducked under the window, cat-footed around to the front with his coat swept back to reveal the Navy Colt holstered on his hip. He pulled the door open and stepped inside, saying, "Hello, Dinger."

Jones, in the process of putting on the trousers, was standing on one leg like a skinny-shanked heron and so startled that he almost toppled over. He managed to remain upright by hopping on the one foot to maintain his balance. His mouth hung slackly open in a blend of surprise, bewilderment, and fear.

"Who the hell're you?"

"Flynn's my name."

"Flynn. Flynn. Christ, you're the bird come around the Red Rooster askin' Mollie about me."

"That's right."

"How'd you find me? Mollie don't know about this place."

"Paddy does."

"Paddy? Paddy who?"

Quincannon moved forward a few paces, into the glow from the lantern so Jones would be sure to see the Navy. "Don't be dense, Dinger. We both know who Paddy is."

Dinger saw the pistol, all right. He pulled his gaze away from it, licked his lips before saying, "He don't go around tellin' birds where to find me. Why'd he tell you?"

"Why do you think?"

"I never seen you before, never heard of you. Paddy never said nothing about nobody named Flynn. What you want with me?"

"Not with you, with the man in charge."

"Huh? Man in charge of what?"

"Taking the Treasury Department for a ride."

"I dunno what you're talkin' about."

"I told you not to be dense," Quincannon said. "The black-leg who makes the queer you and Paddy have been passing."

Dinger pulled on his other pant leg, began buttoning the trousers before speaking again. "Paddy never told you about that," he said.

"Never mind how I found out. I want in on the game."

"Yeah? Why you think you'd get let in?"

"I have a way of passing those counterfeit hundreds in large quantities. Large, quick profits instead of small, slow ones."

"What way?"

"I'll tell that to the man in charge," Quincannon said. "Suppose you introduce me to him."

"Hah. Go talk to Paddy, you think you know so damn much."

"Paddy's not available right now."

Dinger was dim-witted, but not completely devoid of animal

savvy. A light had begun to dawn in his small brain; Quincannon could tell by the tightening of jaw and narrowing of gaze.

"That's right, he ain't. Over in Oakland today. So how could he tell you where to find me?"

"I saw him before he left the city."

"Like hell you did." Dinger's eyes widened with sudden understanding. "You ain't one of us," he said, "you're a goddamn copper!"

Quincannon didn't deny it. Sudden panic seized the scruff; he lunged forward, one shoulder lowered, in a misguided attempt to bowl Quincannon over and flee.

Nimbly, Quincannon sidestepped the blind rush, thrust out a leg that tripped Jones and sent him staggering sideways. Dinger lost his balance, fell atop the table; it collapsed under him in a splintering crash, dislodging the lighted lantern in the process. The glass shattered, spilling oil from the font, which the flaming wick immediately ignited.

Dinger was struggling to disengage himself from the table's remains. Quincannon fetched him a skull clout with the drawn Navy, scotching the effort to rise; a second blow stunned him into immobility.

The burning lamp oil was just starting to spread across the warped floorboards. Quincannon pulled the blanket off the cot, used it to halt the spread of the flames and then to smother them. When he was certain the fire was completely extinguished, he tossed the blanket aside and returned to where Dinger lay twitching now and groaning.

He dragged the mug off the table wreckage, rolled him over onto his back, pulled his arms down at his sides. Then he straddled him at the waist, leaning forward so that his knees pinned the arms to the floor. Dinger's eyelids fluttered, opened halfway with returning awareness. He started to struggle again, spewing fumes of cheap whiskey. Whereupon Quincannon employed a trick he had used before to good advantage. With his left hand he took a firm grip on one of Jones's ears and then inserted the Navy's muzzle into the opposite ear, being none too gentle about it.

Dinger squawked like a frightened parrot, his eyes bulging wide again. His struggles ceased when Quincannon applied wiggling pressure with the tip of the gun barrel.

"In my twenty years as a detective I've killed fourteen men," he lied, "including two who withheld vital information from me. I won't lose any sleep tonight if you're number fifteen."

A strangled noise came from Dinger's throat. His eyes were so distended they might have been on stalks.

"Now then," Quincannon said. "The name of the man running the coney operation."

"Ung . . . ung . . ."

"No man in the world is named Ung. Long Nick Darrow, is it?"

"Who?"

"No, I thought not. His right name, Dinger. You have five seconds before I pull this trigger."

It took only two for Jones to say, "Paddy."

"Paddy? Paddy's the boss?"

"Yeah."

"Is that straight goods?"

"Straight, yeah, I swear."

So then the little snitch Owney had either misheard the conversation in the noisy confines of the Red Rooster, or Lasher had been referring to himself when he said "the boss'll cut your tongue out." Quincannon had been on the trail of the ringleader all along.

"Then who is making the queer?" he demanded.

"Appleby."

"And who is Appleby?"

"Half . . . half brother."

"Paddy's half brother?"

"Yeah. Otto Appleby."

"Printer and engraver, is he?"

"Yeah."

"Located where?"

"Ung . . ."

"Don't start that again." Quincannon screwed the Navy's muzzle another quarter inch deeper, eliciting a bleat of protest. Dinger's voice, when it came again, had an odd scratchy sound, as if his vocal chords had acquired a coat of rust.

"Jesus, my ear . . ."

"Where is Appleby's press located?"

"His shop. Twenty-fourth and . . . Church."

Noe Valley. A respectable, mostly residential neighborhood—the perfect blind for a small-scale coney operation. "And that is where the queer is being manufactured?"

"Yeah."

"How? Using what method?"

"Plates. New ones made from old."

"Old plates. Is that what you found in your mother's trunk?"

"How did you—"

"Never mind that. Answer the question."

"Yeah. In the trunk."

So that was it, Quincannon thought. He'd been wrong after all about Long Nick Darrow's counterfeit plates being destroyed in the warehouse fire. Somehow they'd survived and found their way into the possession of Dinger Jones's aunt in Seattle, where they'd remained for a decade. Just how didn't matter at the moment.

He said, "You found them, gave them to Lasher, and he worked out the counterfeiting scheme with his brother. Is that the way it was?"

"Paddy's idea. Talked Appleby into it."

"And Paddy's in Oakland today, passing more queer."

"Yeah."

Something in Dinger's swift response told Quincannon it wasn't quite the truth. "*Is* he in Oakland?"

"Yeah. Yeah."

"But not passing queer. Doing what over there?"

"I . . . I don't . . ."

Quincannon rotated the Navy's muzzle again. "Doing what?"

"Setting . . . setting up a deal."

"What kind of deal? And don't tell me you don't know."

"With a bird from KC for a bundle."

"A bundle of counterfeit hundreds?"

"Yeah."

No doubt part of a plan to expand distribution of the queer to other cities.

"The bird's name?"

"I don't know."

"Five seconds, Dinger. One, two, three—"

"I swear I don't! Paddy wouldn't say his name."

"All right. Everything you've told me had better be the truth."

Jones swore again that it was. The fear in his eyes and the sweat on his brow confirmed it.

Quincannon removed the Navy, lifted himself onto his feet. He ordered Dinger to roll over onto his belly and clasp his hands behind him. When the scruff obeyed, Quincannon went to where various pieces of finished harness and strips of leather hung on the back wall. He took several of the strips back to where his prisoner lay, straddled him again. Dinger hadn't moved, nor did he now; he was as tame as a frightened puppy. Holstering the Navy, Quincannon tied the mug's hands and then his ankles, securing another strip of leather between the two restraints that drew the legs up into a position rendering him even more immobile.

"Don't bother trying to get loose," he said. "The more you wiggle, the tighter the bonds become."

"You . . . you just gonna leave me here like this?"

"For the time being."

"Listen, Flynn—"

"Quincannon's the name."

"None of this was my idea, see? All I done was pass a few bills. The game's Paddy's, him and Appleby. They're the birds you want."

"And they're two more I'll get. Birds of a feather."

"Huh?"

Quincannon showed him a wolfish grin, picked up his derby from where it had fallen onto the floor, donned it, and took his

221

leave. Outside, to make doubly sure the prisoner would stay put, he snapped the heavy padlock shut through its hasp. Then he hurried around to the rear fence, climbed over and down into the carriageway.

As hot on the trail as he was now, he was more determined than ever to see matters through to the finish on his own. A citizen's arrest of Otto Appleby—and Paddy Lasher, should Lasher have returned from Oakland—and confiscation of the new counterfeit plates, and he would have ended the game as neatly as he had similar ones during his days with the Secret Service. Yaffling Lasher would make the coup perfect, but if such weren't feasible, Mr. Boggs's operatives could take him into custody easily enough.

He didn't miss his time with the Service, but the thrill of the chase to thwart those who sought to defraud the government and the general populace with bogus currency remained strong in his memory. He was in for a tongue-lashing from his former chief, to be sure, but it would be tempered by the success of his actions. And worth it for that reason and his personal satisfaction. Further proof, as if any were needed, that he was the best detective west of the Mississippi, if not in the entire nation.

So thinking, he hurried to the Embarcadero where he hailed a cab to take him to Noe Valley.

25

QUINCANNON

The building on the corner of Twenty-fourth and Church Streets was a low rectangle of pocked, weathered red brick. Electric light showed behind a plate-glass window next to the front entrance on Twenty-fourth; painted on the glass were the words JOB PRINT-ING, with no mention of the proprietor's name. A glance through the window showed no one visible either in front or behind a bisecting counter. From somewhere toward the rear of the building Quincannon heard a steady percussive sound—part metallic thud and part hiss-and-hum. Unmistakably the sound of a printing press in operation.

Adjacent to the building on that side was an awning maker's establishment, an alleyway separating the two businesses. He strolled to the corner and turned it to reconnoiter the Church Street side. A dispenser of paints and varnishes was the print shop's neighbor there, but there was no passageway between the two shops.

Quincannon went back around to Twenty-fourth, crossed the moderately busy street. He stood leaning against a lamppost, pretending to pack his pipe while he debated.

Walk in through the front door as if he were a customer? No. He had no guarantee that Otto Appleby was alone in the shop, and even if that were the case, he would have to put Appleby under the gun in order to gain access to the printing plant at the rear. Someone might enter unexpectedly, or a passerby spy him and his weapon through the window and run for the police. A stealthy approach from the rear was a safer option, one that gave him the element of surprise if he were able to achieve admittance that way.

He recrossed the street. When the sidewalks on both sides were free of pedestrian traffic, he stepped into the alley and followed it to where it emerged into a courtyard just large enough to accommodate a delivery wagon. He listened at a stout rear door recessed into the brick, again heard the thud-and-hiss muted by the thickness of the wall. Inside, he judged, the noise would be loud enough so that whoever was operating the printing press would be unable to hear much of anything else. Pounding on the door to gain the printer's attention was not an option.

His expectation was that it would be securely locked, necessitating the use once more of his trusty set of picks. It might even be barred within, in which case he would have no choice but to enter through the front. But when he pressed down on the latch, the bolt released with a minimum amount of pressure. A dark smile bent the corners of his mouth. Appleby's carelessness made his task that much easier.

Quincannon eased the door open and it swung inward. Any

sound it made was lost in the pounding beat of the press. He widened the opening enough for daylight to penetrate the darkened space inside. Storage room. Cartons of paper, tins of ink, and other material of the job-printing trade were stacked along the walls, the middle of the room free of obstacles between the outer door and a closed inner one.

When he shut himself inside, he was enveloped by thick darkness broken only by a thin rind of light showing beneath the inner door. The distance across to it was a dozen or so paces; he took them carefully, heel to toe, the light strip guiding him. As soon as his extended hands touched the door, he unholstered the Navy.

This latch gave as easily to a downward tug as the outer one had. Quincannon inched the door free of its jamb. The machinery noise, then, was almost deafening. When he laid an eye to the opening, he was looking into a large, open room lit by electric ceiling bulbs. No wonder the new batch of bogus hundred-dollar certificates were of such high quality: the printing press was not one of the old-fashioned single-plate, hand-roller types, but rather a small steam-powered Milligan that would perform the printing, inking, and wiping simultaneously through the continuous movement of four plates around a square frame. Along with its accessories—bundles of paper, tins of ink, a long workbench laden with tools and chemicals—the press took up most of the far half of the room.

The man operating it was middle-aged, squat and sallow-faced, wearing a green eyeshade and a leather apron. Quincannon opened the door a little wider, until the entire room was within the range of his vision. The pressman was its only occupant.

With a clank and a hiss, the Milligan press shut down. The silence that followed the racket was acute. The printer removed what was obviously a batch of finished counterfeit bills from the feeder tray, and when he turned to set them on the workbench, Quincannon stepped through the door with the Navy raised and called out loudly, "Otto Appleby!"

The squat man jumped as if goosed, spun around. The sight of a large, piratically bearded stranger leveling a pistol at him twisted his features into an expression of terrified disbelief.

"Stand fast, Appleby. Hands high."

Appleby flung his hands up with enough force to have wrenched his arms from their sockets. Unlike his half brother, he was no ruffian ready to offer fight or resistance. A mouselike squeak came out of his open mouth, followed by tremulous words.

"Police? You're the police?"

"Worse than that for you. A representative of the United States Secret Service."

Appleby's sallow features lost all color. "I knew it," he moaned, "I knew we'd never get away with a scheme like this. But he didn't give me any choice, he just showed up one day and demanded that I . . . oh, God, I shouldn't have let him bully me into doing it."

Some bunch of crooks these birds were, Quincannon thought disgustedly. A half-wit, a sniveling coward, and a sailor's bane turned thief and purveyor of stolen goods. Bah. Their blasted coney racket had been doomed to failure from the start.

He motioned with the Navy. "Stand away from the bench."

Appleby obeyed, his movements as shaky as his voice and his

upthrust hands. Quincannon crossed to the bench, picked up one of the counterfeit notes, held it up to the light.

"Tolerably good work," he said. "How did you manage such accomplished bleaching and bill-splitting?"

"The other bills, they showed me how."

"What other bills?"

"The old ones he gave me."

"Paddy gave you—Paddy Lasher, your half brother."

Convulsive head bob. And another self-pitying moan.

"Counterfeits. Made from old-fashioned engraved zinc plates."

"Yes."

"How many were there?"

"Not many. Half dozen."

There was no need to ask where Lasher had gotten the bogus notes. Dinger Jones must have found a small cache of them in the trunk along with the anastatic plates. That explained how Appleby had been able to manufacture counterfeits approximating the quality of Long Nick Darrow's: he had simply studied the original plates and used them as a model for his new set. A talented printer and forger in his own right, to his everlasting sorrow.

Quincannon said, "How many new bills have you made?"

"Only . . . only a few hundred."

"Where are the rest?"

"In that carton there on the floor."

"Paddy must have taken some with him for his rendezvous in Oakland. A bundle or a just a few samples?"

Appleby squeezed his eyes shut before saying, "Christ, you know about that, too."

"A bundle or a sample?" Quincannon repeated.

"Sample."

"When do you expect him back?"

"No particular time. He wasn't sure how long the meeting would take."

"But he will be coming here?"

"I think so. Do you—"

"Intend to wait for him? That remains to be determined. Who has charge of the genuine cash accumulated from passage of the counterfeits? Paddy?"

"No. He left it with me."

"Trusting soul, eh? Where is it?"

"The safe in my office."

"Does Paddy have the combination?"

"Yes. Just him and me."

"Let's have a look."

The office was a boxlike enclosure sandwiched between the printing room and the customers' section. Appleby knelt before the safe, an old black Mosler, Bahmann, and fumbled shakily with the combination lock. It took him several tries to get the door open.

The spoils were a mix of stacked greenbacks and bagged gold eagles and double eagles. A fair lot of both—enough to tell Quincannon that there were quite a few more bogus notes in circulation than Mr. Boggs's estimate.

"How much is here, Otto?"

"I . . . I'm not sure," Appleby said.

"Yes you are. Paddy would have kept tabs and so would you. How much?"

"Almost eight thousand."

"And your share? One-third?"

Appleby's eyes glittered briefly, a residue of greed. "More," he said. "An even split with Paddy."

"What about Dinger Jones?"

"A smaller share. Twenty percent. He . . . he didn't like it, but he's afraid of Paddy."

So was Appleby. Fear of his bullying half brother as much as the lure of illicit riches was what had toppled him from the straight and narrow.

Quincannon ordered him to close the safe and then to change the combination, a precaution against Lasher getting his hands on the loot before Mr. Boggs's operatives could confiscate it. That done, he herded Appleby back into the printing room.

There was a pair of ink-stained gloves on the workbench. Quincannon holstered his weapon—Appleby was no threat to attack or flee—and picked up and donned the gloves. Then he backed away to the Milligan press, located and detached the new set of counterfeit plates. Back by the bench, he found a piece of burlap sacking in a waste barrel and wrapped the plates in it. He slid them into his coat pocket, then removed the gloves.

"The zinc plates," he said then. "Where are they?"

"I destroyed them. He told me to."

"And the old counterfeit notes?"

"Those, too."

"Well and good. Now then, we—"

Quincannon broke off because Appleby's gaze shifted away from him, eyes widening, jaw hinging open. That was enough to alert him. He was pivoting, reaching again for the Navy, even before he heard the scrape of a boot sole on the linoleum floor.

He had a swift glimpse of the thick-mustached, black-suited brute who had emerged from the front part of the shop, the leveled pistol in his hand thrust forward at arm's length. Quincannon was starting to crouch and dodge, his own pistol only halfway free of the holster, when Paddy Lasher fired.

The bullet brought a sharp cut of pain as it slashed close along the side of Quincannon's head. Appleby shouted something that was lost in the roar of a second shot. That one missed entirely, for Quincannon had thrown himself to the floor. He landed on his left shoulder and rolled, clearing and lifting the Navy, as Lasher's pistol cracked for the third and last time, his aim once again poor.

Quincannon's aim was far better. The Navy bucked twice and both rounds found their mark. Blossoms of blood appeared on the front of Lasher's vest; he staggered, fell hard enough to his knees to jar the weapon from his clutch, and toppled forward on his face.

Appleby ran to his half brother's side, leaned down as if to touch him, then quickly pulled his hand back. His face was ashen now. "You killed him," he said, but the words were without emotion of any kind.

Quincannon slowly picked himself up. He was aware of warm wetness on the side of his head and neck, of throbbing pain in the vicinity of his left ear, but his first thought was of Lasher and Lasher's pistol. He went to gather and then pocket the weapon. Lasher still hadn't moved; his head was turned just enough so that one staring eyeball was visible. Dead, right enough.

Appleby continued to stare down at the corpse. He said dully, "He must have come in while we were in the office and heard us talking. He always did walk soft."

Quincannon only half heard him. *Fired upon twice in the space of a single week,* he was thinking, *one would-be assassin wounded and one dead in retaliation. Two close calls, this one very close. Too damned close.* He reached up an exploring hand, felt the sticky wetness of blood matting his beard and trickling down his neck into his shirt collar. His fingers traced a furrow of burned and bloody flesh along the hairline. Wincing, he touched the ear—and a small, cold tremor passed through him.

The earlobe was missing. Lasher's first bullet had torn it off.

He fished out his handkerchief, pressed it tight to stanch some of the blood flow. "Appleby," he said. "Appleby!"

The printer blinked, turned his head, blinked again. "You're bleeding."

"That's right, blast you. Do you keep any medical supplies here? Carbolic acid, iodoform, bandages?"

"It looks as though you need a doctor—"

"Medical supplies! Yes or no?"

"Yes. For emergencies—"

"What the devil do you suppose this is. Where are the supplies?"

They were in a small room opposite the office containing a cot and other furnishings; evidently Appleby lived as well as worked on the premises. Quincannon dampened a large ball of cotton with carbolic acid. When he applied it to the wounds, he was forced to bite down hard to keep a pain-cry locked in his throat.

Another soaked cotton ball, a gauze pad, and strips of adhesive tape made a temporary makeshift bandage.

"Where is the nearest doctor?" he demanded then.

"Two blocks from here."

"Good. Take me there. Don't try to run away—you'll regret it if you do. And don't say a word to the doctor when we get there. I'll do the talking."

"What about Paddy?"

"He's not going anywhere," Quincannon growled. "We are. First to the doctor's office, then to the U.S. Mint. Now move!"

26

SABINA

She was worried about John.

He hadn't been the same in the two weeks since his single-handed cracking of the counterfeiting ring. There had been little of his usual ebullience at the successful culmination of an investigation, his explanations to her relatively brief and lacking in dramatics. He'd become quieter, more withdrawn in a brooding kind of way. Part of the reason, she supposed, was that Mr. Boggs, while grateful for the results, had expressed in no uncertain terms his disapproval of John's "vigilante tactics" in obtaining them.

But she suspected that a larger part of the reason was John's brush with death. She had been horrified when she saw the wound in his scalp, the missing earlobe; the knowledge that Paddy Lasher's bullet had come within a fraction of ending his life was chilling. He had attempted to brush off the near miss, terming it another in a long line of occupational hazards. He had been wounded before in the heat of battle, he said, and survived with no lasting ill effects. Which was quite true, yet she sensed that this encounter had had a more profound effect on him than any other except the accidental shooting of the pregnant woman in Arizona.

He kept self-consciously fingering his damaged ear, as if he couldn't quite believe the lobe, a small piece of himself, was gone and could never be replaced. The deformity, small though it was, embarrassed him, too; now that the bandage had been removed, he sought to cover the ear with an unbecoming beaver hat in place of his usual derby. A constant reminder of how near he had come to perishing.

For most of his adult life he had been courageous to a fault. This had led to his reckless behavior, for he had convinced himself that he was fated not to die in the line of duty as his father had—and as Stephen and so many others in their profession had. Now, it seemed, the once iron-willed belief had been shaken; that this narrow escape had finally made him realize he was not indestructible after all, forced him to confront his mortality. Whether the effect would be permanent or not remained to be seen. If the incident made him wiser, more cautious, and less cocky, then that was all to the good. What concerned her was that it might have an adverse effect, erode his skills and his self-confidence and render him less effective.

She attempted to draw him into talking about his feelings, but neither direct nor subtle overtures succeeded. The lack of success only made her more determined. If he remained uncommunicative and morose, she would take drastic measures. Just what those measures might be she wasn't sure yet. Not quite sure, anyway.

But it might not come to that. The first indication that he might be ready to emerge from his shell came late Friday afternoon of the third week. Since returning from a routine insurance claim investigation, he had been sitting tilted back in his desk chair, smoking his pipe and lost in thought. When she brought him out of his reverie by informing him that it was nearly five o'clock, he tilted forward, touched his ear, and said without preamble, "Have dinner with me tomorrow evening, Sabina."

It was the first social invitation he had tendered since his close call. "Oh," she said lightly, "are you finally going to honor your promise?"

"Promise?"

"Of dinner in payment for my interviewing Dinger Jones's mother. You do remember?"

"I remember."

"The name of the restaurant I suggested, too?"

"Delmonico's."

"Yes. Delmonico's."

Sabina expected a whimper if not a bleat of protest, and was prepared to substitute a less expensive selection, but John didn't bat an eye; she might have suggested a food cart at the nightly Market Street bazaar for all the reaction he exhibited. He merely nodded and said, "I'll call for you at seven o'clock."

Curious, Sabina thought. Normally his invitations were put forth with smiles, banter, terms of endearment. This one had been solemn and earnest, as if there were more to it than a desire to spend a pleasant evening out with her.

QUINCANNON

Delmonico's was a purveyor of French cuisine, arguably the finest such fare in the city. Onion soup, sole meunière, *coquilles Saint-Jacques, blanquette de veau,* and for dessert, the house specialty of fried cream flambé. Sabina ate with her usual hearty appetite, but Quincannon picked at and barely tasted any of the dishes. It was an effort to maintain polite, much more so intimate, dinner table conversation. His mind wandered, his nerves felt so tightly strung he could almost hear them twanging. And he couldn't seem to stop fingering his mutilated ear, which he was sure every other diner in these opulent surroundings had noticed when he removed his hat and was covertly studying.

The multicourse meal, one he would have enjoyed in different circumstances and in spite of the outrageous prices, seemed interminable. Sabina, always sharp-eyed and intuitive, noticed his discomfort, of course. Twice she asked if he was feeling well, and twice he assured her that he was in fine fettle—half-truths that sounded false even to him.

When she had finished the last of a large portion of the rich fried cream, she sighed contentedly, dabbed at her lips with her linen napkin, and said she believed she had just enough room for a cup of café au lait. The last of Quincannon's patience evaporated at this. He leaned forward, reached out to touch her hand.

"My dear, we needn't have it here."

"No? Where, then?"

He drew a deep breath. "At my flat."

"Ah. Your flat."

"I have no designs on your virtue," he said, and was unable

to resist the urge to dandle his ear again. "There is something important I want to discuss with you."

"Why can't we discuss it here?"

"Best said in complete privacy. And the night is too cold for a buggy ride or a long walk. Will you come?"

He managed not to fidget while she studied him for what seemed like a long time. Finally, to his relief, she said, "Yes, I'll come."

A hansom delivered them, none too soon to suit Quincannon, to his rooms on Leavenworth. The one time Sabina had been there previously she had commented on his seductive—her word—taste in furnishings, especially the large gilt parlor mirror adorned with mostly nude naiads that he'd purchased on a whim. This time she said nothing, simply perched on the velveteen settee after allowing him to take her wrap.

"You needn't bother with coffee, John."

"Brandy instead? Sherry?" He kept bottles of both on hand for his lady visitors, when he'd had lady visitors other than Sabina.

"Nothing, thank you. Just tell me what's on your mind. You're as nervous as a cat tonight."

He sat down beside her. His collar felt tight; he resisted the urge to loosen it, fingered his ear instead. His mouth was very dry. "I have been doing quite a lot of thinking," he said. "You and I . . ."

"Yes?"

"You and I . . . well, we've been together, partners, for six years now—"

"Almost seven."

"Yes, almost seven. And we have been keeping company outside the office for nearly a year now—"

"Eight months, to be exact."

She was not making this any easier for him. He coughed to clear his throat, started over. "Life is short, and we've reached a point when . . . ah . . . when neither of us is getting any younger—"

"So good of you to remind me!"

"I didn't mean that the way it sounded," he said hastily. "I only meant . . ." What had he meant? His mind seemed to have gone temporarily blank. He shook his head. "Sabina . . ."

"Yes?"

"Sabina . . ."

"Yes, John?"

"Sabina . . ."

"For heaven's sake, what is it?"

Now his collar felt very tight. "I've given this a great deal of thought and I . . . have something to ask you."

"Go ahead, then."

"Will you . . ." The words seemed to clog in the vicinity of his esophagus. *Say it, you blasted dolt! Say it before you choke on it!*

And say it he did, after another harrumph to clear his voice box. "My dear Sabina, will you do me the honor of becoming my wife?"

She stared at him for several seconds and then burst out laughing.

He was taken aback. "You find the proposal amusing?" he said with wounded dignity.

"No, no. I'm sorry, my dear, I couldn't help it. The expression on your face, like a little boy with a bad tummy ache . . . oh, my."

"Faugh. Does that mean your answer is no?"

"On the contrary," she said. "I accept your proposal, John Frederick. Of course I'll make an honest man of you."

She kissed him soundly, passionately. And then she stood, and to his utter astonishment, she took his hand and led him into his own bedroom.